Bachelor Girl

The ROSE *Years*
By Roger Lea MacBride
Illustrated by Dan Andreasen
& David Gilleece

LITTLE HOUSE ON ROCKY RIDGE
LITTLE FARM IN THE OZARKS
IN THE LAND OF THE BIG RED APPLE
ON THE OTHER SIDE OF THE HILL
LITTLE TOWN IN THE OZARKS
NEW DAWN ON ROCKY RIDGE
ON THE BANKS OF THE BAYOU
BACHELOR GIRL

Bachelor Girl

Roger Lea MacBride

Illustrated by Dan Andreasen

HarperCollins*Publishers*

*To Foster Winans, builder of his own little house,
with profound gratitude and respect*

Harper Collins®, ♣®, Little House®, and The Rose Years™
are trademarks of HarperCollins Publishers Inc.

Library of Congress Cataloging-in-Publication Data
MacBride, Roger Lea, 1929–
    Bachelor girl / Roger Lea MacBride ; illustrated by Dan Andreasen.
        p.   cm. — (Little house)
    Summary: Having left her parents' Missouri farm for good and trained
to become a telegraph operator in Kansas City, teenage Rose moves out
to San Francisco and joins the thousands of "bachelor girls" supporting
themselves.
    ISBN 0-06-027755-6. — ISBN 0-06-028434-X (lib. bdg.)
    ISBN 0-06-440691-1 (pbk.)
    1. Lane, Rose Wilder, 1886–1968—Juvenile fiction. [1. Lane, Rose
Wilder, 1886–1968—Fiction. 2. Telegraph—Fiction. 3. Kansas City
(Mo.)—Fiction. 4. San Francisco (Calif.)—Fiction] I. Andreasen, Dan,
ill. II. Title. III. Series.
PZ7.M12255Bac 1999   99-10604
[Fic]—dc21   CIP
                                                                  AC

1   2   3   4   5   6   7   8   9   10

First Edition

Dear Reader:

The book you hold in your hands is the work of my father, Roger Lea MacBride. It continues the childhood story of Rose Wilder Lane, and her mother and father, Laura Ingalls and Almanzo Wilder. Rose treated my father much as she would have treated a grandson and told him many stories about what it was like growing up in Missouri almost a hundred years ago. Dad took those stories and spun them into a series of books based on the facts of Rose's life. Bachelor Girl *is the eighth and last of those books.*

I'm sorry to have to tell you that my father has passed away. But my sadness is softened some because his work, the stories of Rose's early life, has continued. He left four partially completed manuscripts that continue Rose's tale, right up to the time she is seventeen years old and has left home to start a life of her own.

With the help of the editors at HarperCollins, we have been able to complete the story of Rose and her family as they come into the modern age of the telephone and automobile.

I am very pleased that these stories will be

available to new generations of readers. You will find, as I did, that in a hundred years the things young people think and worry about haven't changed all that much.

Abigail MacBride Allen

Contents

Back Home   1

A Good Start   21

Left Behind   34

On Her Own   54

Give Me a Chance   65

Bachelor Girl   81

A Real Celebration   94

If I Had a Little Money   108

Call Me Miss Wilder   129

The Big City   143

New Friends   161

This Is the Life!   172

A Game Little Kid   186

When We Are Married   201

A Surprise Visit   217

Life Begins Anew   232

Back Home

On a sweltering June afternoon, soon after she had returned home from Louisiana, Rose paused in the shade of the post-office doorway, leaned against the jamb, and sighed. Her eyes swept Mansfield's main street, drowsing in the hazy midday sun. She prayed to see something new, something different—anything that would catch her interest.

She looked, as she had a thousand times before, upon the rickety wooden awnings over the sidewalks. The usual loafers sat in tipped-back chairs on the porch of the Mansfield Hotel, spitting tobacco juice into the dust. A group of boys clamored like a flock of crows as they pitched horseshoes under the oak tree in front of the blacksmith's shop. Those same boys, it seemed, had been doing that since Rose could remember. A whiff of manure floated over from the livery stable.

The grass in the park across the street was mangy, in need of mowing. The paint on the gazebo, fresh and snowy white when Rose had celebrated the start of the new century four years before, had cracked and peeled. A broken spindle leaned out from the balustrade like a loose tooth. With shingles missing from the roof, the once-proud gazebo put her in mind of a forgotten, battered old doll.

She sighed again. Nothing of importance had happened in Mansfield for years. She would be glad, she thought, to never see the town again. She did not want to stand there looking at it. But she also did not want to follow the stale road home to the old farmhouse, which had somehow shrunk since she was little.

Rose was only seventeen years old, yet already she felt her life was wasting away.

She knew she should be doing something. But the weight of the slow, uneventful days stole her will. It was the same feeling she had when she stayed in bed too late, knowing she should get up yet not having the energy.

She had to do something with her life, but she did not know what.

Rose had been home just two weeks from her fall and winter in Crowley, Louisiana. Those had been the best months of her life. She had lived with her dear aunt Eliza Jane; she had graduated high school with high honors; she had worked for the causes of socialism and women's rights; she had shaken the hand of the great Eugene V. Debs and heard him speak; and she had learned new languages and new cultures. She had even been courted by a handsome, dashing college man from Chicago.

Still, when graduation was over, she was

ready to return to the little town in the Ozarks. She had missed the comforts of home: the sound of Mama's voice, the smell of Papa's pipe, the cozy rhythms of the everyday life she'd known since the day she was born.

When she'd first stepped off the train, Rose had fallen into the arms of Mama and Papa, so happy and grateful to be back that she'd burst into tears. Until she'd set eyes on them, she hadn't known how much she'd missed them.

Mama had written to Rose that she and Papa had moved back onto Rocky Ridge Farm, a mile outside town. For many years— Rose had lost count—the family had lived in town because the farm couldn't support them. They had lived in a house in town, where Mama took in boarders. Papa had worked as a drayman. He still delivered coal oil for Mr. Waters, but now he spent more of his time tending the apple orchard, the fields, and the livestock.

It had been a thrill to return to the little

house she had lived in when the family had first emigrated to Missouri from South Dakota in 1894. Of course, the house was grown up now, with a second-floor attic bedroom and real windows and a drain in the sink so Mama didn't have to carry her dirty dishwater outside. But it was still in the same spot, just on the edge of the ravine where the ever-flowing spring ran.

Rose took to her old chores gratefully, glad for the freedom from having to fuss every day with her hair and dresses. She could even go barefoot. What a joy to feel the earth under her feet again! In Crowley, a big bustling city of 5,000 souls, she hadn't dared step out of Aunt Eliza's house without a clean shirtwaist and polished shoes.

On the farm it was just the three of them, as it had been all those years before, and a hired man who came in several times a week to help Papa with the heavy work.

It was also a comfort, at first, to be back among the farm animals. Feeding the chickens and having them jostle eagerly at her feet for their mash made her feel like some great, indulgent mother hen. It was good to be back milking the cow and spilling a little for the kittens. Brushing the horses, fetching wood for the stove, even sweeping the floor—all were small acts of love for the simple life of her past.

Little had changed, except that poor old Fido, the black-and-tan terrier that had wandered into their campsite ten years ago when they had first arrived in Missouri, had passed away while Rose was in Louisiana. She had grown up with Fido, and his absence was a missing note in a familiar tune.

Mama and Papa had gotten a new dog, an Airedale they named Nero. Nero had wiry, dull-brown hair, walked on legs as stiff as sticks of wood, and barked at everything, which made Rose miss Fido all the more. But he was a good ratter and not afraid to kill snakes.

During the first week of her return, Rose caught up with old friends and schoolmates on her errands in town. She went for long walks around the farm with Papa, listening as he gave his opinions on the apple orchard, weather, and crop prices.

In the immaculate, cozy kitchen, Rose spent time with Mama, kneading the bread dough while Mama peeled potatoes. Rose and Mama chattered away, barely stopping for breath, enjoying the cooling breezes that came in through the screened windows.

They traded news of the past three seasons and discussed the important issues of the day: votes for women and the presidential election that would be held that fall.

One day Rose was setting the table for noontime dinner when she caught Mama gazing at her wistfully, the wooden spoon she'd been stirring the beans with stopped in midair.

"What is it, Mama?"

"What happened to my little girl?" Mama asked wonderingly. "Look what a poised young woman you've become! Why, it seems only yesterday I had to scold you for scuffing up your good shoes. Where did my little girl go? Where did all that time go?"

Rose beamed as she brushed a stray crumb off the tablecloth into her palm. "Thank you, Mama. And you look as beautiful as ever."

"For an old lady." Mama chuckled. She put the lid back on the pot with a clatter and opened the oven door to check the biscuits.

To Rose's eyes Mama was not anything like an old lady—even if she was all of thirty-seven years old. Mama still stepped quickly around the kitchen, her hands still fluttered expertly over her sewing, her voice was still full of energy and life. Best of all, her eyes still sparkled, and she still whistled when she was content.

"You never seem any older to me," said Rose. "You never change a bit."

Mama brushed back a strand of her hair, which was brown but streaked with gray at the temples. "I may not look it, but believe me when I say I feel it."

Seeing the little town in the Missouri Ozarks with fresh eyes, Rose at first had been taken by how quiet and restful it was. She had felt safe in its arms, grateful to be back.

But after the first week, she and Mama began to run out of things to talk about. Several days of heavy rain turned all the roads to thick mud, making it hard to get to town. Rose was reminded of how lonely she'd often felt growing up on the farm. She began to miss the pleasure of walking to an ice cream parlor, or buying fresh bread as she had often done in Crowley, or hearing the Acadians speaking French on the street corners.

It was the modern age, and what did Mansfield have to show for it? Folks talked about getting an electric illuminating plant, but no one wanted to pay for it. There were telephones, but not at Rocky Ridge Farm. Even if Mama and Papa could have paid for one, the only people to call were the ones they saw every day in Mansfield.

No one dared bring a locomobile to town. The roads were so rocky and rutted, the machines would be battered to bits if they didn't get bogged down in the mud first.

The Opera House had a show now and

then, but mostly plays or minstrel shows Rose had already seen in Crowley's busy theater. Of course, there were ice cream socials and pie suppers to attend. But Rose discovered she hadn't very much in common with the young ladies in town.

Rose's best friend, Blanche Coday, was off living with relatives in Chicago, attending finishing school. The other girls she'd known in school were either getting engaged and married now, talking about colicky babies and how high eggs had gotten, or getting settled in their ways, like the old maids they seemed certain to become.

The older women gossiped about one another's clothes and families. Rose wondered what they said about her and Mama when their backs were turned.

None of the women in town seemed to care whether or not they ought to have the right to vote, or about the terrible conditions in the cities, or about the plight of the working man.

Rose felt as if she had never been away, except that before leaving she had wondered what she was missing in life. Now she knew, and that knowledge was beginning to smother her.

There *was* Paul Cooley, the young man whom she was sure she would marry one day. His letters were a great comfort. But Paul was far away in Illinois, working as a telegraph operator for the Western Union Company, and at times marriage to him seemed as unreal and impossible as a dream. Paul's mother had used up almost all the insurance money from his father's death on the railroad. Now Paul had to send money home to support her.

It would take some time for him to save enough for him and Rose to settle down together. Unless Rose could find work, to earn some of her own money . . . But what could she do in such a small place as Mansfield? She began to worry she'd wind up an old maid.

In the doorway of the post office Rose sighed a third time, tucked the day's mail in her market basket, and wondered what had happened to her life. Everything had come to

a standstill, and she had no idea what to do about it.

A long purple curl of smoke unfurling over the apple orchards on Patterson's Hill was the plume of Number Five coming in. Men sauntered past, going toward the depot. The postmaster appeared in his shirtsleeves, pushing a wheelbarrow filled with mail sacks down the middle of the street.

The afternoon hack from Hartville rattled by, bringing a couple of tired, dust-grimed drummers. The town girls—bareheaded, laughing, talking in high, cheerful voices— came hurrying from the post office and the drugstore to see Number Five come in. That was the big entertainment in Mansfield— watching the trains come into town. Rose had loved to meet the trains when she was a young girl. Now it seemed so foolish.

Rose shifted the weight of the package on her arm, pulled her straw boater farther down to shade her face, and started home.

She passed the wide, empty doorway of the livery stable and the glowing forge of the blacksmith's shop without seeing them, absorbed in the turmoil of her thoughts.

But at the corner where the gravel walk began and the street became a country road slipping down a little slope between scattered white cottages, her thoughts were shattered by a man's voice crying out her name. Startled, Rose turned and looked back down the street, toward the town square.

A young man was running at full tilt toward her, his hand holding his hat on his head. Rose gasped. Paul Cooley! He had stepped right out of her thoughts, become flesh and blood out of thin air!

Her heart began to beat quickly. She stood there rooted to the ground in shock. Her spirit soared. She blushed. She was wearing an everyday dress, a crisp but faded calico. She had done her hair up hastily and could feel her chignon coming loose. She hated for Paul to see her such an awful wreck.

Every lace-curtained window behind the rosebushes along the sidewalk suddenly seemed to conceal watching eyes, and the

sound of Paul's feet scattering the gravel
was loud in her ears. He reached her at last.
Winded, his face red and damp, he fought to
catch his breath.

"Hello, Paul," Rose said in astonishment.
"I . . . I was just thinking of you." It had been
more than a year since she had seen him.
He'd become a young man, muscular, dark-
haired, with blue eyes. Rose thought him
even more handsome than she remembered.

"Rose, dear," Paul gasped. "Had no . . .
time to wire. I just . . . got in on Number . . .
Five. Gosh, Rose. You look . . . so pretty.
A sight for . . . sore eyes."

The flutter at her heart stopped. No, she
was not pretty. Whenever she looked in a
mirror, her features were too large, her forehead too high. The eyes in the mirror were
gray, and the hair was straight and brown.
Not even a pretty light brown, as it had been
when she was younger.

She despised the face that looked back at
her. She longed for tiny, pretty features, large
brown eyes, a low forehead with curling hair.

But Paul had come home to her anyway.

They walked slowly on the road out of town under the arch of the trees. The sun sent long, slanting rays of light between the branches. There was a colored haze over the orchards, and the hills were freshly green from the rains.

"Well, I've quit my job," said Paul, self-consciously stuffing his hands in his pockets.

"Quit your job?" Rose was shocked. Paul had had a good assignment in Rock Island, a busy depot. "But, why? What will you do?"

"I didn't just up and quit. We were going to strike, Rose. The telegraphers' union. Everyone had joined, and we were voting whether to strike. At one of our Sunday meetings a spy was there, and on Monday morning the chief operator had a complete list of everyone who attended. As soon as I saw them start lopping men off, I hiked."

They reached the top of the hill that separated Rocky Ridge Farm from town. Down below in the shallow valley ran Wolf Creek. On the other side, partway up the hill in one of the fields, Rose could see Papa hoeing between the rows of young corn. From a distance he looked old and stooped, like the man in the famous poem "The Man with the Hoe."

"What will you do?" Rose wondered. She felt a wave of panic in her chest. Without a job Paul would never save enough to marry.

"I can get another job," he said. "But maybe I can find something close to Mansfield, maybe in Springfield. That's a big depot, only sixty miles from here. Don't you worry. Things will work out."

"I wish I had a job," Rose declared. "I know I could, if I only had the chance." Rose had thought about becoming a telegrapher. More women were getting work as operators all the time.

"Gee, I hate to see a girl go to work," said Paul. His lips were full and very firm. When he set them tightly, as he did now, he looked determined. There was something wonderfully strong about the line of his chin and the slight frown between his heavy black brows. Rose's whole being seemed to melt and flow toward him.

Even though she knew she could work, and wanted to, she didn't want to seem quarrelsome. She kept her thoughts to herself, preferring to bask in the glow of Paul's presence, which had come just when she had needed it so much.

"Remember when we explored the cave under Patterson's Hill?" Rose said, pointing across the hillside to the place where the cave entrance was hidden behind a clump of trees.

"Oh, my gosh!" Paul cried out, his face lighting up. "I clean forgot about that. We were just a bunch of kittens back then. Remember how we ran screaming for the entrance when the torch went out? Holy smokes, that was a long time ago."

It was many lifetimes ago, Rose thought. How many times they had walked along this road together!

"It must be awfully lonely, living in towns

where you don't know a soul," Rose said. Paul had been assigned to several different depots since he had become an operator. He was never anywhere for more than half a year or so.

"It's not so bad," said Paul. "It'd be swell . . . I mean, someday . . . Well, there's lots of folks who support themselves doing what I do. Up at Rolla there's a man and his wife who handle the station between them. He works nights and she works daytimes. They live over the depot, and if anything goes wrong, she can call him."

"That must be nice," she said. It did sound cozy.

"He's pretty lucky, all right," Paul agreed. "It isn't exactly like she's working, of course—right together like that. I guess maybe they couldn't have been married un- less she did work. He didn't have much, I reckon. You know, he isn't so awfully much older than— But anyway, I'd hate to see— anybody I cared about going to work," he finished desperately.

They stopped halfway down the hill, under a tree. The grasshoppers whirred noisily in the grass. The clink of Papa's hoe echoed from across the creek. Paul looked across the valley as if deep in thought. Rose was afraid to speak for fear she'd say the wrong thing.

Finally Paul took his hat off and mopped his brow with his handkerchief. "I'd best be getting on to Mother's house, Rose. I saw Mrs. Banks in front of the post office, and I'm sure the word has spread that I'm back. I don't want to worry her.

"Look here," he quickly added. "If I get a buggy next Sunday, what do you say we go driving somewhere?"

Rose carried those words home with her, singing as she went.

A Good Start

Rose had been ready and waiting that Sunday afternoon long before she heard the sound of harness jingling from across the valley.

All morning she had been in her room. She had tried to do her hair in a new way, putting it up in rag curlers the night before, working with it for hours in the stuffy attic bedroom in front of the wavy mirror, combing it, putting it up, taking it down again, with a nervous fluttering in her wrists. In the end she gave up. She rolled the long braid into its

usual mass at the nape of her neck and tied on
a black ribbon bow.

She longed for a new white dress to wear
that day. The lawn she'd worn in Crowley,
fuzzy along the hem from so much walking,
seemed raggedy to her as she contemplated it
stretched in all its freshly ironed stiffness on
the bed. But it was the best she could do.

While she dressed, the sounds of the warm,
lazy summer day floated in to her through the
half-open window. The whinnying of the long-
legged colt in the barnyard, the answering
neigh of his mother from the pasture, the
cackling of the hens blended like the notes of
a pastoral orchestra.

The murmur of her father's talk with a
neighbor in the barnyard came up to her. She
heard, without listening, the sounds running
together into a pleasant hum of contentment.

When she had pinned her collar and put on
her straw sailor hat, she stood for a long time
gazing into the eyes that looked back at her
from the mirror, lost in a reverie.

"Gracious!" Mama said when Rose finally

appeared in the kitchen. "What're you all dressed up for, this time of day?"

"I'm going driving," she answered with a pang of guilt. Mama stopped, the oven door half open, a fork poised in her hand. Rose hadn't mentioned her plans to Mama. She hadn't wanted to answer any questions about her and Paul's future.

"Who with?"

"Paul, of course."

Mama paused, then turned back to the stove.

"Well," she said, closing the oven door, "even if you are going out with a beau, that's no reason you shouldn't eat something. Dinner won't be ready till two o'clock, but you ought to drink some milk anyway."

Rose answered that she was not hungry. Paul would come by one o'clock, she thought. Mrs. Cooley had only a cold lunch on Sundays.

He came ten minutes after one, and Rose had forgotten everything else in the strain of waiting.

She met him at the gate, and he got out to help her onto the buggy seat. He was wearing his Sunday clothes: the blue suit, carefully brushed and pressed, and a stiff white collar. He looked strange and formal.

"It isn't much of a rig," he said apologetically, clearing his throat. She recognized the bony sorrel and the rattling buggy, the cheapest in the livery stable. But even that, she knew, was an extravagance for Paul.

"It's hard to get a rig on Sunday," she said. "Everybody takes them out in the morning. I think you were very lucky to get such a good one. Isn't it a lovely day?"

"It looks like the rains are about over," he replied in a polite voice. After their first glance they had not looked at each other. He chirruped to the sorrel, and they drove away.

Protected from the warm sun by the roof of the buggy, they saw before them the yellow road winding among the trees, disappearing, appearing again like a ribbon looped about the curves of the hills. There was gold in the green of the fields, gold in the poppies beside the road, gold in the ruddiness of young apricot twigs. The clear air itself was filled with vibrant, golden sunshine. They drove in a golden haze.

What they said did not matter. The only thing that mattered was being together.

Paul's arm lay along the back of the buggy seat. Its being there was like a secret shared between them. Rose expected nothing more. Paul had tried to kiss her once when she was younger. But it hadn't been the right time, so she had refused him. Paul had been the perfect gentleman, as he had as long as she had known him.

Finally, by a grassy hill, they left the buggy, tying the patient sorrel in the shade beneath a tree. They clambered up the hillside to gather wildflowers.

Paul took Rose's hand to help her up the trail, and she permitted it, although she could have climbed more easily by herself. She was glad to feel that he was the leader, content that he should think himself the stronger.

At the top of the hill they came to a low-spreading live oak with a patch of young grass beneath it, and here, forgetting the ungathered flowers, they sat down.

They sat there a long time, Paul talking very seriously on grave subjects: life and the meaning of it, the bigness of the universe, and how it makes a fellow feel funny, somehow, when he looks at the stars at night and thinks about things.

Rose understood. She felt that way herself sometimes. It was amazing to learn how many things they felt in common. Neither of them had ever expected to find anyone else who felt them, too.

Then there was the question of what to do with your life.

"It's a pretty important thing to decide," Paul said earnestly. "You don't want to make mistakes, like so many men do. You have to start right. That's the point, the start. When you get to be twenty or so, like me, you realize that, and you look back over your life and see how you've wasted a lot of time already.

You realize you'd better begin to do something."

Paul plucked a leaf of furry mullein and rubbed it between his fingers.

Telegraphy would provide a good future, they agreed. Somehow, then, they began to talk as if Rose would be with him.

"I might be a telegrapher too," Rose dared to say. Paul was silent, so she went on.

"Wouldn't it be fun if I were, so we could be in the same town? You'd help me with the train orders, and if you worked nights, I could fix your dinner for you."

They made a sort of play of it, laughing about it. They were only supposing, of course. Rose kept from speaking the thought that clamored behind everything she said, that set her heart racing and kept her eyes from meeting his, the thought of that young married couple at Rolla.

When the afternoon was gone, and only a golden western sky remained behind the flat, blue mass of the hills, they stood reluctantly, hesitating. Paul had taken Rose's hands to help her to her feet. In the grayness of the twilight they looked at each other.

Paul drew Rose closer. She felt a strong current sweeping her away. She let him put his arms around her and hold her for a long moment. She didn't want to kiss him yet, and he didn't try. Her cheek against his suit jacket, she could feel the pounding of his heart.

"Well, then," Paul finally said in a husky voice. "Your mother'll be worrying by now."

Their hands clung for a moment, uncertainly, then dropped apart. They stumbled down the dusky trail and drove home in silence.

The days after that became like notes in a melody. Linnets' songs and sunshine stream-ing through the attic windows, or gray panes and rain on the roof—they were all the same to Rose. Each day seemed like a holiday. Rose slipped from beneath the patchwork quilt and dressed with eager fingers; life was too good to be wasted in sleep!

She seemed made of energy as she ran down the steep stairs to the kitchen. Life and hope swelled in her veins as a flooding river frets against its banks in spring.

Every sight and sound struck upon her senses with a new freshness. There was exhilaration in the bite of cold water on her skin when she washed in the tin basin on the bench by the door. The smell of coffee and frying salt pork was as good as a banquet. She sang while she spread the red tablecloth on the kitchen table and set out the plates.

> *"You're as welcome as the flowers in*
> *Ma-a-ay,*
> *And I love you in the same o-o-old way."*

It seemed to her that she was caroling aloud poetry so beautiful that only she could appreciate it. She walked among her parents and the folks in town as if alone, wrapped in a glory no one else could see.

One afternoon, when the ironing was finished, Rose dressed in her pink gingham and best shoes. She was going to town for the mail, she told Mama. When Mama said, "Why, you went day before yesterday!" Rose replied, "Well, I guess I'll just go to town, anyway. I feel like walking somewhere."

Mama accepted the explanation without further comment. The blindness of other people astonished Rose. It seemed to her that every blade of grass in the fields, every scrap of white cloud in the sky knew that she was going to see Paul.

She let her hand rest a moment on the gate as she went through. It was the gate on which they leaned when he walked her home from church on Sunday nights. She could feel his presence there still; she could almost see the dark form of his shoulders against the starry sky, and the pale blur of his face.

The long lane by the meadow was crowded with memories of him. Here they had stopped to gather poppies; there, just beside the gray stone, he had knelt one day to tie her shoe. On the little bridge over Wolf Creek, shaded by the oak trees, they always stopped to lean on the rail and watch their reflections shot across by ripples of light in the stream below.

She was dazzled by the beauty of the world as she went by all these places. It seemed to her that she had been blind all her life.

She stood some time on the little bridge, looking at all this loveliness, and she said his name to herself, under her breath: "Paul." A quiver ran along her nerves at the sound of it.

Rose knew Paul would be busy handling baggage at the railroad station when she got to town. He had gotten himself a temporary job, beneath his abilities but something to bring in a bit of money until a more solid job came along.

Rose thought of his sturdy shoulders in the blue work shirt, the smooth forehead under his ragged cap, the straight-looking blue eyes, and the firm lips. She would stand a little apart, by the window where the telegraph keys were clicking, and he would pass, pushing a hand truck through the crowd on the platform. Their eyes would meet, and the look would be like a bond unseen by the people who jostled them.

Then she would go away, walking slowly

through the town, and he would overtake her on his way home to supper. Her thoughts went no further than that. They stopped with Paul.

But before she reached town, Rose saw little Sammy Harner frolicking in the road. He skipped from side to side, his wide straw hat flapping. He shied a stone at a bird. He whistled shrilly between his teeth. When he saw her, he sobered quickly and came trotting down the road, reaching her, panting.

"I was coming out to your house fast as I could," he said. "I got a note for you." He sought anxiously in his pockets, found it in the crown of his hat. "He gave me a nickel and said to wait if they's an answer."

Excited, she tore open the railway company's yellow envelope and read:

Dear Friend Rose:

I have got a new job and I have to go to California tonight, where I am going to work. I would like to see you before I go, as I do not know when I can come back, but probably

*not for some time. I did not know I was going
till this afternoon and I have to go on the
Cannonball tonight. Can you meet me about
eight o'clock by the bridge? I want to see you
very much. Please answer by Sammy.*

Your friend, Paul

The familiar surroundings were suddenly
unreal. Rose felt light-headed. "Tell him I
didn't have a pencil," she said. "Tell him I said
yes." And as Sammy lingered, watching her
with curiosity, she added sharply, "Hurry!
Hurry up now!"

It was a relief to sit down when at last
Sammy had disappeared around the bend in
the road. The whirling world seemed to settle
somewhat into place then. She had never
thought of Paul's going away. She wondered
in her numbness if it was a good job, and if he
was glad to be going.

Left Behind

She came down the road again a little after seven o'clock. The road lost itself in the twilight before her, and the fields stretched out, as endless as the sky. She knew she was early, but she could not wait in the house another minute.

For an eternity she walked up and down the road, stumbling in the ruts, waiting. She went as far as the top of the hill beyond the bridge and saw shining against the gathering blackness the yellow lights of Paul's house. She looked at them for a long time. At last she saw him coming, and she stood still in the pool of darkness under the oaks until he reached her.

"Rose?" he said uncertainly. "Is it you?"

"Yes," she answered. Her throat ached.

"I came as quick as I could," he said. Somehow she knew that his throat ached too. They moved to the little railing of the bridge and stood trying to see each other's faces in the gloom. "Are you cold?" he asked.

"No," she said. She saw then that her shawl had slipped from her shoulders and was dragging over one arm. The wind fluttered it, and her hands were clumsy, trying to pull it back into place.

"Here," he said, taking off his jacket.

"No," she said again. But she let him wrap half the jacket around her. They stood close together in the folds of it. The cool evening wind flowed around them like water, and the warmth of their trembling bodies made a little island of coziness in a sea of cold.

"I've got to go," he said. "It's a good job. Ninety dollars a month. I've got to support

Mother, you know. Her money's pretty nearly gone already, and my brother, George, off who knows where. I've got to go. I just wish—I wish I didn't have to."

Rose tried to hold her lips steady. "It's all right," she said. "I'm glad you've got a good job."

"You mean you aren't going to miss me when I'm gone?" Paul sounded worried.

"Yes, I'll miss you," Rose said quickly.

"I'm going to miss you an awful lot," he said mournfully. "You're going to write to me?"

"Yes, I'll write if you will."

"You aren't going to forget me—you aren't going to get to going with anybody else—are you?"

Rose could not answer. The ache in her throat dissolved into tears, and they clung together in voiceless misery.

"Oh, Rose! Oh, Rose!" He held her tight. "You're so—you're so—sweet!" he stammered, and then they kissed for the first time.

If only that moment could go on forever,

Rose thought, miserable knowing it could not.

"I don't want you to go away," she sobbed.

His arms tightened around her, then slowly relaxed. His chin lifted, and she knew that his mouth was setting into its firm lines again.

Tears were welling slowly from Rose's eyes and running down her cheeks. She was not able to stop them.

"I have to," Paul said. The finality of the words was like something solid beneath their feet once more.

"Yes," Rose said halfheartedly. "I've got to do something to help at home too." She groped for the shawl, which had slipped from her shoulders again. He picked it up and wrapped it carefully around her.

A new solemnity had descended upon them both. Rose felt dimly that life had changed for her, that it would never be the same again.

They walked up and down in the starlight, trying to talk soberly, feeling very grown-up and sad, a weight on their hearts. He was going to be a night operator at the station in Sacramento, the capital of California. It was a big depot, a busy, important town full of busy, important people. It was a good job, and pretty soon maybe he would be able to get a better one. It wouldn't be long to wait before he'd have saved enough money.

They were clinging together again at Rose's gate. The memory of the times they had stood there before was the last unbearable pain.

"You—haven't said—tell me you—love me," Paul said after a long time.

"I love you," Rose told him for the first time. Saying it was a sacred vow. Paul was silent for another moment, and in the dim starlight she saw a strange expression on his face.

"Would you go away with me—right now—and marry me? If I asked you to?" His voice was hoarse.

"Yes," she said.

"If—if only we could!" he said mournfully.

They kissed again. Then Paul was going down the road, almost running, and soon the darkness hid him.

Left Behind

* * *

In the days that followed, it seemed to Rose that she could have borne the separation better if she had not been left behind. Paul had gone down the shining lines of track beyond Patterson's Hill into a vague big world that baffled her thoughts.

Paul's first letter came less than a week later. He wrote that he had been in San Francisco and taken a ride on a sight-seeing car. It was a splendid place, he said. He wished Rose could see the things he had seen: Chinatown, the Presidio, the beach, and Seal Rocks.

Then he had gone on to Sacramento. The work was good, he was well and hoped she was, and he thought of her every day and was hers lovingly.

But Rose felt that she was losing touch with him. When she thought about two or three years of waiting, she felt that she would lose him entirely. She thought again of that young couple at Rolla, and pangs of envy were added to the misery in which she was already living.

Mama tried to be a comfort, indulging Rose's broodiness and offering hopeful words of wisdom: "A boy always returns to his first love." She tried to interest Rose in a day trip to Hartville, or a church picnic. But Rose said she was not good company for anyone. She wanted to be alone and cling to the hurt.

Besides, there was nothing anyone could say or do that would change the cruel truth that Rose felt more trapped now than she had been before Paul had come home.

She had had this feeling before. Her future always seemed to lie out there somewhere, just beyond her reach.

Several weeks after Paul had gone, Rose was walking home from the post office, flipping through the pages of the weekly *Mansfield Mail*. Her eyes snagged on a notice for a school of telegraphy in Kansas City. Her heart began to pound. She sat down on a rock in the hot sun and read it over and over again.

It said, "Operators in great demand. Graduates earn $75 to $100 a month and up. Inquire about our reasonable tuition rates." Her head swam with possibilities.

As soon as she got home, she dashed upstairs and secretly wrote to that school. She didn't want to debate it with Mama, or hear about the cost of sending her, or the scandal of a single girl going off to the city to live among strangers. She didn't want to hear anything except yes.

Rose could barely keep her nerves in check, waiting to hear back. Mama and Papa noticed right away that her spirits had risen. She did all her chores cheerfully, and even helped Papa in the barn cleaning out the stalls, a job she hated.

"I'm glad to see you have taken control of your life again, Rose," said Mama. "Things will come out right. You'll see."

A reply came a few days later. The letter assured her that she could learn everything she needed to know in three months, that railroad and telegraph companies were clamoring for operators, that the school guaranteed all its graduates good positions.

The tuition was fifty dollars. Just looking at that number, with the dollar sign in front of it, gave Rose a stomachache. She trembled as she walked home that day from the post office, the letter tightly clamped in her hand.

Mama was just setting supper on the table when Rose walked in. Papa sat in the chair by the door, pulling off his muddy boots.

Rose wanted to wait to speak her piece until they had all sat down. But if she didn't get it out, she thought she'd jump right out of her skin.

"I'm going to be a telegraph operator," she declared.

Mama put a fresh towel in the breadbasket and dumped the biscuits from their pan into it. Then she neatly folded the towel over the biscuits to keep them warm.

Papa grunted as he pulled off his second boot. He stood and began washing his hands in the basin.

Rose watched them with growing amazement.

"But . . . but—aren't you surprised?" she

cried out. "Aren't you going to say anything?"

"No, I'm not surprised," said Mama, setting the biscuits on the table and pulling out
her chair. They all sat down. Papa glanced at
Rose with a twinkle in his eye. Rose was even
more confused.

She pulled the letter from her apron pocket.
She unfolded it with trembling hands and
wordlessly slid it across the table to Mama.

Mama picked it up and set it down between herself and Papa, and they read it
together.

"Fifty dollars," Papa said, shaking his nearly
bald head. "It's a fortune to live on for just
three months."

Finally the dam that had been holding back
all her thoughts and feelings burst.

"I know it's a lot of money, Papa. I thought
about that. But I would pay it back. You know
I would. As soon as I get my first job. Look, it
says right there that they *guarantee* a job for
every graduate. Think of the wages I'd earn,
and the money I could send home. I couldn't
help at all if I stay here. There's nothing in

Mansfield for me. I'd be a good girl. I'd write every day. I'd . . ."

On and on she went, and Mama and Papa listened patiently. When she realized she was repeating herself for the third time, Rose fell silent, clasped her hands in her lap, and stared into her plate like a little girl waiting to be scolded.

"Eat now, Rose," Mama said kindly. "You've gotten yourself so worked up lately, you're looking thin.

"We knew you wrote to that school," Mama went on. "Ella Sims told me. She heard it from Myrtle Miller, who heard from Mrs. Boles, the postmaster's wife. I suppose she saw the letter before it went out."

"Oh!" Rose scowled. "I just hate the gossip in this town!"

Mama and Papa had talked things over already and decided that if Rose wanted it as much as that, well, they would find a way for her to go.

"I checked with Craig at the bank," Papa said, wiping his mustache with his napkin.

"I'll be renewing the mortgage for another year in a few days. I can borrow an extra hundred dollars for tuition and expenses."

Rose was too stunned to speak at first. Finally she stammered, "I thought you'd never . . . I mean, well . . . I thought for certain you'd try to talk me out of it."

"If I thought I could, I would," Mama said, her blue eyes full of love. "I'm worried. And I'm sad to think of you leaving again, so soon after you got home. But you are even more headstrong than I was at your age. You're old enough to make your choices."

"Oh, Mama. Papa," Rose nearly sobbed. "I'm sorry. I didn't mean . . ."

"We know you didn't," Papa said, patting Rose's hand. "We know there's a bigger world out there. It's different now from when your mother and I were coming up. You should have your chance to try your luck, if you've a mind to."

It was settled then, just like that.

It had been so swift, Rose worried maybe she was being too hasty. But she knew she could not bear to sit in Mansfield any longer, feeding chickens and dodging gossip, waiting for Paul.

In the next days Mama went over Rose's clothes with her. She gave Rose her telescope bag in which to pack them.

A new closeness grew up between them as they worked. Mama said it was just as well for Rose to have a good job and be a bachelor girl for a while. Maybe Rose wouldn't make a bad mistake in getting married before she was sure she knew her own mind, as some girls did.

"But I want you to promise me: If anything comes up that looks as if it isn't just right, you let me know right away," Mama said. "I'm going to be worried about you, off alone in a city like that."

Rose promised quickly, and Mama began to talk of something else: Mrs. Updike, who lived on the next farm, was going out to San Francisco to visit her sister. Mrs. Updike would go with Rose as far as Kansas City and see her settled there before she continued her journey.

Left Behind

Mama said Rose must be sure to eat her meals regularly and keep her clothes mended and write every week and study hard. Rose promised all those things.

There was a flurry on the last morning. Rose repacked her bag three times to be sure that nothing was left out.

Mama and Papa drove her to town, crowded into the two-seated light wagon. There was another flurry at the depot, where they met Mrs. Updike. Then the train came in.

Rose hugged Mama and Papa awkwardly, smiling with tears in her eyes. She felt, as she had many times before, how deeply and completely she loved them. And then Rose was on the train and the train was moving, and Mama and Papa slid from sight. It was the second time Rose had left Mama waving her handkerchief on the platform.

Rose gazed back at Mansfield, and the little yellow station where Paul had worked, until the train rounded the curve west of town. Then she settled back against red-velvet cushions to watch unfamiliar trees and hills flashing backward past the windows. She had a sense of adventure, wondering what the school would be like, promising herself again to study hard.

It took most of the day to reach Kansas City. Rose and Mrs. Updike fretted that by some mischance Mr. Weeks, the manager of the school, would fail to meet them at the station. They wore bits of red yarn in their buttonholes so that he would recognize them.

He was waiting when the train stopped. He was a young, thin, well-dressed man, with a face that seemed strangely old, like a half-ripe apple that had withered. He hurried them through the noisy, bustling streets, on and off streetcars, up a stairway at last to the school.

There were two rooms: a small one, which was the office, and a larger one, bare and not very clean, lighted by two high windows looking out on an alley. In the large room were half a dozen tables, each with a telegraph sounder and key on it. There was no one there at the moment, Mr. Weeks explained, because it was Saturday afternoon. The school usually did no business on Saturday afternoons, but he would make an exception for Rose.

If she liked, he said briskly, she could pay him the tuition now, and begin her studies early Monday morning.

Rose obediently opened her handbag and pulled out the precious envelope she had carried all the way from Mansfield. She handed it to Mr. Weeks, knowing that she could not turn back now.

Mr. Weeks popped the envelope into his pocket without so much as a look at it.

"I'm sure you will be a good operator, Miss Wyler," he said. Rose would have corrected him, but she thought it might seem rude. She wanted to make the best impression.

Mr. Weeks guaranteed Rose a good position when she graduated. He would even give her a written guarantee if she wished.

But she did not ask for that. It would have

seemed to imply a doubt of Mr. Weeks' good faith.

Mrs. Updike, panting from climbing the stairs and nervous with anxiety about catching her train to Denver, asked him about rooms. He knew a very good and cheap rooming house, next door to the school. He was kind enough to take them to see it.

There were a number of rooms in a row, all opening on a long hallway reached by stairs from the street. They were kept by Mrs. Brown, who managed the restaurant downstairs. She was a pale young woman, with very bright brown eyes and yellow hair. She talked continuously in a light, falsely cheerful voice, making quick movements with her hands and moving about the room that was to be Rose's with a whisking of silk petticoats.

Mrs. Brown apologized for a tear in the chair seat. "I'm recently a widow," she said. "It's about all I can do just to keep up the rooms and run the restaurant downstairs."

The room rented for six dollars a month.

It had a large bow window overlooking the street, brightly flowered wallpaper, a red carpet, a big wooden bed, a washstand with pitcher and bowl, and two rocking chairs.

At the end of the long hall was a bathroom with a white tub in it. Rose thought there was something sophisticated about tubs; a bath in one was always an event far different from the Saturday-night scrubs in the tin washtub at home.

And Rose could eat in the restaurant below, said Mrs. Brown; very good meals for twenty cents, or even less if she wanted to buy a meal ticket.

"I guess it's as good as you can do," said Mrs. Updike, checking her watch.

"I think it's lovely," Rose said.

So it was settled. Rose gave Mrs. Brown six dollars, and she whisked away after saying, "I'm sure you'll like it, dearie, and if there's anything you want, let me know. I sleep right in the next room, so nothing's going to bother you, and if you get lonesome, just come and knock on my door."

Then Mrs. Updike, with a hasty farewell peck on Rose's cheek, hurried away to catch her train. Mr. Weeks went with her to the station, and Rose was left alone.

She locked her door first, and counted her money, feeling very businesslike. She had exactly the $44 that would pay for the rest of her room and board for the next three months. She also had another $7.40 that Mama had given her at the last minute for "extras."

Then Rose unpacked her bag and put away her things, pausing now and then to look around the room that was now hers. It seemed very large and luxurious. She felt a pleasant sense of responsibility when everything was neatly in order, and she stood at the window, looking down the street to the corner where she saw streetcars passing.

She promised herself to work very hard and to soon pay back the money Mama and Papa had lent her, with interest.

Then she thought, smiling, that in a little while she would go downstairs and eat supper

Left Behind

in a restaurant. Then she would buy a tablet and pencil and, coming back to this beautiful room that was now her own, she would sit down and write a letter to Paul.

On Her Own

The thought of Paul was Rose's anchor while she stumbled through the first weeks in Kansas City. It was the only thing that warmed her in the midst of the strangeness that surrounded her.

She did not know what she had expected of the school, but she didn't think she'd found it. Faithfully every morning at eight o'clock she was at her table in the dingy back room, struggling to translate the dots and dashes of the Morse alphabet into crisp, even clicks of the sounder. It took Rose the longest time just to

54

be able to make a short click sound different from a long one. Learning just the right touch was very difficult. She practiced the alphabet until her hand ached from gripping the sounder knob so tightly.

There were two other pupils, farm boys who moved their necks uncomfortably in stiff collars and reddened when they looked at her. Rose could see that although they came from the same sort of background as she did, she was not like them at all.

There was a wire from the students' room into the front office. Sometimes its sounder opened with a click, and they knew that Mr. Weeks was going to send them something to copy. They moved to that table eagerly. But then the sounder did not click again. After a while one of the boys would tiptoe to the office and report that Mr. Weeks was asleep.

On other days the sounder would tap for a long time meaninglessly, while they looked at each other in bewilderment. Then it would make a few shaky letters, stop, then make a few more.

For several days Mr. Weeks did not come to the school at all. Rose and the other students sank into a kind of stupor, sitting in the warm room not knowing what to do, while flies buzzed on the windowpane.

Rose's damp fingertips stuck to the hard rubber of the key; it was an effort to remember the alphabet. But she kept hard at work, even when Mr. Weeks was asleep or absent, knowing how much depended upon her success.

Always before her was the vision of the station where she would work with Paul, a little yellow depot with housekeeping rooms upstairs. She thought, too, of the debt she owed Mama and Papa, and the help she could give them later when she was earning money.

Bit by bit she learned a little about the other pupils. Their names were James and Richard, and they had come down from St. Joseph, Missouri, together. They had worked two summers to earn the money and had been able together to save only seventy-five of the one hundred dollars for their tuition.

But they had been sharp enough to persuade Mr. Weeks to take them for that sum. They lived together in one room at a hotel along tne waterfront and cooked their meals over the jet of the gaslight.

One of the two boys, Richard, had a more knowing air than the other. He smoked cigarettes and he swaggered a little, as though he were a man of the world and knew all the wickedness of the city.

He looked at Rose with eyes she did not like, and once he asked her to go to a moving-picture show with him. Although she was very lonely and had never seen a moving picture, she refused. She felt that Paul would not like her to go.

Rose spent her free time reading at a library near the office or writing letters in her room. Sometimes she walked along the streets marveling at the noise, the beautiful goods in store windows, the thousands of lives about which she could only wonder.

Yet at the end of three months in Kansas City, the only people she knew were Mr.

Weeks, the two other students, and Mrs. Brown.

She felt that she would like Mrs. Brown if she knew her better. Her shyness kept her from saying more than "Good evening" when she handed her meal ticket over the restaurant counter to be punched. And Mrs. Brown, though always pleasant, was far too busy to do more than nod back.

It was her own fault, Rose decided. Mrs. Brown laughed and talked merrily with the men customers, cajoling them into buying cigars and chewing gum from her little stock in the glass counter.

Rose wondered about Mr. Brown. She wondered what he might have been like. Mrs. Brown often looked at her wide wedding ring, turning it on her finger. A widow so young! Rose's heart ached at the thought of that brief romance.

Mrs. Brown's thin figure and bright-yellow hair were those of a girl; only her eyes were old. Rose thought it must be grief and worry that had given them that hard, weary look.

Rose smiled at her wistfully over the counter, longing to express her friendliness and sympathy.

Rose tried to make her three-dollar meal ticket last a month. That meant only five times a week could she sit in luxury, eating warm food in an atmosphere thick with smells of coffee and stew and hamburger steak.

The rest of the time she ate in her room. Cinnamon rolls could be bought for half price on Saturday nights, and she kept a bag of them, and some fruit. It was the only way to make her money last, but she always felt a little uneasy when she saw Mrs. Brown's anxious eye on the vacant tables. She felt that she was cheating Mrs. Brown somehow by eating in her room.

Mrs. Brown worked very hard, Rose knew. It was she who swept the hall and kept the rooms in order. She did not do it very well. She swept with quick, feverish strokes. Her yellow hair straggled over her face; her heels clicked on the floor; her petticoats made a whisking sound. She looked exhausted.

There was something so piteous about her that each night Rose stole down the hallway, taking the broom from its corner as if she were stealing it instead of borrowing, and secretly swept and dusted her own room.

Somehow it made Rose feel better that she was giving Mrs. Brown a bit less to do. She wished that it took more time. When she had finished, there was nothing to do. So she sat at her window, looked down at the street, and practiced the Morse alphabet with her fingers tapping on the sill.

People went up and down the sidewalks, strolling slowly in the warm summer evening. She saw girls in dainty dresses, walking about in groups, and the sight increased her loneliness. Buggies went by: a man with his wife and children out driving, a girl and her sweetheart.

At the corner there was the clanging of streetcars, and she watched them passing, brightly lighted, filled with people. Once in a while she saw a locomobile. Her breath quickened and she leaned from the window to keep it in sight until it was gone. She felt the charm of the city, with its crowds, its glitter, its strange, hurried life.

Two young men often passed down that street in a locomobile. They looked up at her window when they went by and slowed the machine. If Rose was leaning on the sill, they would wave to her and shout.

She always pretended that she had not seen them and drew back. But she watched for the machine to pass again. It seemed to be a connection between her and all the exciting life from which she was shut out.

Rose sat at the window one evening near the end of the three months that she had planned to spend in the telegraph school. Paul's picture was in her hand. He had had it taken for her in Sacramento and sent it in the mail. It was a beautiful shiny picture, cabinet size, showing him against a tropical background of palms and ferns.

He had taken off his derby hat, which he held somewhat self-consciously. He had an air of prosperity about him, and it wasn't just the new suit he was wearing. His head was turned so that his eyes did not quite meet hers. It was baffling, that cool gaze. It even hurt a little. She wished that he would look at her. She felt that the picture would help her more if he would, and she needed help.

Mr. Weeks had returned from one of his long absences that day, and she had taken courage to ask him about the job he had guaranteed. He had listened while she stood beside his desk, stammering out her worry and her need.

She thought she telegraphed pretty well; she had studied hard. Her money was almost gone. She watched his shaking hand fumbling with some papers on his desk and felt that she should not bother him when he was sick. But desperation drove her on.

She did not suspect the truth until he looked up at her with reddened eyes and answered with slurred words. Then she saw that he was drunk. The shock came upon her in a wave of nausea.

Mr. Weeks pulled a piece of printed paper

from a cluttered pile, signed his name to it, and handed it to Rose.

"Here's your certificate of graduation," he muttered. "Someone'll hire you with that."

She trembled so that she could hardly get down the stairs. She walked a long time in the clean sunshine trying to make sense of it all.

When she reached her room at Mrs. Brown's, she sat at the window and confronted the awful truth.

She could hope for nothing from the telegraph school. And she had just two dollars, a half-used meal ticket, and a week left before she had to pay rent again.

Her mind ran desperately from thought to thought, like a caged creature seeking escape between iron bars.

She could not go home. She could not live there again, defeated, knowing day by day that she had added a hundred dollars to Mama and Papa's mortgage. And she could not go to Paul. She had told him so confidently that she could do as well as a boy if she had the chance, and she had had the chance. She could not ask him to help her.

The street below was full of people going by, absorbed in their own concerns, careless of her predicament. She felt herself falling into the bottomless depths of despair.

Give Me a Chance

The next morning Rose dressed very carefully in a fresh white shirtwaist and her best skirt and went down to the Western Union office to ask for a job.

She knew where to find the office. She had often looked at its plate-glass front lettered in blue during her lonely walks on the crowded street. Her heart thumped loudly, and her knees were weak when she went through the open door.

The big room was divided by a long

counter, on which a young man lounged in his shirtsleeves, a green eyeshade pushed back on his head. Behind him telegraph instruments clattered loudly, disturbing the stifling quiet of the hot morning. The young man looked at her curiously.

"I would like to speak with the manager, please," said Rose.

"Manager? Won't I do?" he asked.

She heard her own voice, trying to keep up the courage in it.

"I'd rather see him. If he's busy, I could wait."

The manager rose from the desk where he had been sitting. He was a tall, thin man, with sparse hair combed carefully over the top of his head. His lips were thin, too, and there were deep creases on either side of his mouth, like parentheses. He said his name was Mr. Roberts.

Rose explained that she was looking for a job.

"I'm sorry, I don't need another operator," he said. But he paused and gazed curiously at

Rose for a moment. "What experience do you have?"

She was a graduate of the Weeks School of Telegraphy, she told him breathlessly. She could send perfectly; she wasn't so sure of her receiving, but she would be awfully careful not to make mistakes.

"I just have to have a job," she pressed on frantically. "I just have to have a job. It doesn't matter how much it pays. . . . Anything will do!"

Rose could not walk out of that office without the promise of some work. She clung to the edge of the counter as if she were drowning and it were a lifeline.

"Well, come in. I'll see what you can do," he said.

Rose could have burst into tears with gratitude at even this small chance.

He swung open a door in the counter, and Rose followed him through, then between several tables. On a battered desk, back by the big switchboard, was a dusty sounder. The manager took a message from a hook on the wall and gave it to her. "Let's hear you send that."

Rose began, being painfully careful. The young man with the eyeshade wandered over. He stood leaning against a table, listening. After she had made a few letters, she caught him nodding to the manager over her head.

She finished the message. She thought she had done very well. When she looked up, the manager said kindly, "Not so bad! You'll be an operator someday."

"If you'll only give me a chance," she pleaded.

The young man turned away and, sitting down, began to send a pile of messages, working very busily, sending with his right hand and marking off the messages with his left. Rose was astonished at his speed.

"Well! And you want to work here?" The manager rubbed one hand over his chin, smiling. "I don't know. I might."

"Oh, if you would!"

He hesitated for an agonizing moment.

"Well, I'll think about it. Come and see

me again." They shook hands, and she left.

She felt that he was very kind. She felt, too, that she had conducted the interview very well, and a ray of hope warmed her while she walked back to her room.

When she got back to her room, Rose wrote her weekly letter to Mama and Papa, saying that she had finished school and was about to get a job. She hesitated a long time, with her pen in midair, before she added that she did not have much money left and could she borrow another five dollars. She promised to pay it back with the rest.

She had eaten a stale roll and an apple and was figuring how long she could make the meal ticket last when she heard a knock on her door.

She opened it in surprise, thinking there had been a mistake. A stout, determined-looking woman stood there, a well-dressed woman with black gloves and a veil.

"You're Rose Wilder? I'm Mrs. Campbell." She stepped into the room and swept the place with one look. "What on earth was your mother thinking of, leaving you in a place like this? Did you know what you were getting into?"

"I don't know . . . What . . . Won't you take a chair?" said Rose, baffled.

Mrs. Campbell sat down gingerly, very erect. They looked at each other.

"I might as well talk straight out to you," Mrs. Campbell said. "I met Mrs. Morris, Mrs. Updike's sister, at the Eastern Star convention in St. Louis last week, and she told me about you, and I promised to look you up.

"Well, when I found out! I told Mr. Campbell I was coming straight down here to talk to you. If you want to stay in a place like this, well and good, it's your affair. Though I should feel it my duty to write to your mother." She brushed a speck of dust from her knee.

"I wouldn't want my own girl left in a strange town, at your age, and nobody taking any interest in her."

"I'm sure it's very kind," Rose murmured in bewilderment.

"Well"—Mrs. Campbell drew a long breath

and plunged on—"I suppose you know your mother would never approve of your living in such a place?"

A wave of confusion went through Rose's mind.

"Everybody in town knows that this place Mrs. Brown runs is nothing but a flea trap," Mrs. Campbell continued, not even bothering to lower her voice. Rose cringed with embarrassment.

"Everyone knows she lets her rooms to the sort of people a respectable girl oughtn't to have anything to do with. Drifters, tramps, women who have no good reason to be traveling alone. I don't know what this world is coming to when . . ."

Mrs. Campbell went on in her sharp, forceful voice. Rose half heard the words, wanting to ask her to stop talking.

She felt that everything about her was being poisoned. She wanted to escape, to hide, to feel that she would never be seen again by anyone. When Mrs. Campbell finally stopped, it was hard for Rose to speak.

"But what will I do?" she said in a small voice.

"Do? I should think you'd want to get out of here just as quick as you could."

"But where can I go? My rent's paid. I haven't any money."

Mrs. Campbell thought for a moment.

"Well, you will have a job, won't you? Your folks don't expect you to live here on nothing, do they? If it's only a day or two, I could take you in myself rather than leave you in a place like this. There's plenty of decent places in town. You ought to be able to find one in a few days.

"The first thing to do is to pack your things right away. How long is your rent paid? Can't you get some of it back?"

Rose dutifully began to pack her things, moving about in a fog of confusion and misery.

Mrs. Campbell stood by the door, watching like a hawk while Rose packed. She did not stop talking, and Rose tried to answer her in a thankful-sounding tone.

When Rose had managed to cram all her
things into the telescope bag, they went
down the stairs. Mrs. Campbell waited outside the restaurant while Rose went in to ask
Mrs. Brown to refund the $1.50 she had paid
for the coming week's rent. It was noon, but
there were only one or two people in the
restaurant. When Rose stammered that she
was leaving, Mrs. Brown's smile faded.

"You are? What's wrong? Anybody been
bothering you?"

"No," Rose said hastily. "That is, it's been
very nice here, and I liked it, but a friend of
mine, she wants me to stay with her. I'm sorry
to leave, but I haven't much money."

She struggled against feeling pity for Mrs.
Brown. She choked over asking her to refund
the rent, feeling it was almost an act of cru-
elty. But Mrs. Campbell was watching her.

Mrs. Brown said she could not do it.
"House policy," she said abruptly. "No re-
funds."

She did offer to give Rose something in
trade, though, $1.50 worth. She tried to make

the trade seem businesslike, but Rose wanted just to flee.

Her eyes swept the cigars and candy in the glass counter. At a loss and wanting this moment to be over quickly, she pointed to a heap of peanut brittle candy. She had often looked at it and wished she could afford to buy some. Mrs. Brown's thin hands shook, but she was piling the candy on the scale when Mrs. Campbell came in.

"What's she doing?" Mrs. Campbell asked Rose, her eyebrows arched. "You buying candy?"

"I don't know what business it is of yours, coming interfering with me!" Mrs. Brown broke out. Then she turned to Rose. "You tell her if I'm not keeping a decent, respectable, quiet place and doing the best I can and minding my own business and try- ing to make a square living." Her voice was high and shrill. Tears were rolling down her face. But she went on breaking up the candy and piling it on the scales. "I don't know what I ever did to anybody. You'd think folks would have a little pity."

"I didn't come here to talk to you," snapped Mrs. Campbell. "Come on out of here," she commanded Rose. Rose blindly took the sack of candy and marched out the door, which Mrs. Campbell slammed behind her as they left.

Hurrying to keep pace with Mrs. Campbell's furious haste down the street, Rose was overwhelmed with shame and confusion. She felt terrible for poor Mrs. Brown, who hadn't asked to be made a widow and have to fend for herself. The whole affair was like a splash of mud upon Rose, too. Suddenly it was as if she had done something wrong.

When they were on the streetcar, safely away from it all, Rose's awkwardness grew still more, and she felt it in Mrs. Campbell as well. Mrs. Campbell looked at Rose, at the bulging telescope bag, the shabby shoes, and the faded sailor hat, and Rose felt the gaze like the glow from a hot stove. She knew that Mrs. Campbell was wondering what on earth to do with her.

Pride and helplessness choked her, and she could not think of anything to say. She knew Mrs. Campbell must think her sullen, but she couldn't help herself. Mrs. Campbell's impatient tone was jabbing at Rose like a sharp stick.

Mrs. Campbell lived in splendor in a three-story white house on a quiet street. The smoothness of the well-kept lawns, the clean lines of the swept cement walks cried out against Rose's shabbiness. She had never been so aware of it.

When she was seated in Mrs. Campbell's parlor, oppressed by the velvet upholstery and the piano and the beaded portieres, she tried to hide her shoes beneath the chair and did not know what to do with her hands.

She answered Mrs. Campbell's questions about the telegraphy school and Mr. Weeks because she had to. But she felt that the last coverings of her self-respect were being torn from her.

Finally, Mrs. Campbell threw her hands up

and said, "The thing for you to do is to go home."

"No," Rose said. "I . . . I can't do that."

Mrs. Campbell looked at her curiously, and Rose felt the heat flaming in her cheeks. She could not discuss the renewed and increased mortgage on the farm, the money she owed Mama and Papa.

Mrs. Campbell sighed. "Well, I suppose you can stay here a few days."

Rose lugged the telescope bag up the stairs. The wooden steps shone like glass. Mrs. Campbell showed her a room at the end of the hall. A mass of things filled it: children's toys, old baskets, a broken chair.

It was like a closet, but larger, with a tiny window at one end. It was large enough to hold a narrow white iron bed, a washstand, and a chair, and still leave room to swing the door open. These furnishings appeared when Mrs. Campbell had dragged out the other odds and ends.

Watching her swift, efficient motions in

silence, Rose tried again to feel gratitude. But the fact that Mrs. Campbell expected it made it impossible. She could only stand ever more awkwardly, longing for the moment when she would be alone.

When at last Mrs. Campbell went downstairs, Rose shut the door quickly and softly. She wanted to fling herself on the sagging bed and cry, but she did not.

She stood with clenched hands, looking into the small, blurred mirror over the washstand. A white, tense face looked back at her with burning eyes. She said to it, in a determined whisper, "You're going to do something, do you hear? You're going to do something quick!"

Some time later she heard the shouts of children and the clatter of pans in the kitchen below. It was almost suppertime. She took a cinnamon roll from the paper sack in her bag, but it was so dry and stale, she could not eat it. She was looking at it when Mrs. Campbell called up the back stairs, "Miss Wilder! Come to supper."

She braced herself and went down. It was a good supper, but she could not eat very much. Mr. Campbell sat at the head of the table, a stern-looking man who said little except to speak sharply to the children when they were too noisy.

There were two children, a girl of nine and a younger boy in a sailor suit. They looked curiously at Rose and did not answer when she tried to talk to them. She decided they had been told to leave her alone.

When she timidly offered to help with the dishes after supper, Mrs. Campbell told her that she did not need any help. Her tone was not unkind, but Rose felt put off. Fearing she would cry, she went quickly upstairs.

She looked at Paul's picture for some time before she put it back into her bag, where she thought Mrs. Campbell would not see it. Then, sitting on the edge of the bed under a flickering gas jet, she wrote him a long letter.

She told him that she had moved. Describing the street, the beautiful house, the furniture in the parlor, she drew such a picture of comfort and happiness that as she reread it, the feeling of her words warmed her somewhat. Her life might not be perfect, but she could make it seem perfect by writing it that way.

It was a beautiful letter, she thought. She read it over several times before she carefully turned out the gaslight and went to bed.

Bachelor Girl

Early the next morning she went to the Western Union office and pleaded again for a job. Mr. Roberts, the manager, was very friendly, talking to her for some time and encouraging her to come back. Something might turn up.

She went back every morning for a week, and often in the afternoons. The office almost became a home for her, a place where she found hope. The rest of the time she walked about the city or sat on a bench in the park.

Rose didn't like taking charity. She felt so

uncomfortable when she ate Mrs. Campbell's food that several times she did not return to the house until after dark, when she was sure that they would be finished with their supper. She had to ring the doorbell, for the front door was kept locked. Each time Mrs. Campbell asked her sharply where she had been. Rose always answered politely.

Rose now understood from experience the old saying that another man's bread is hard to swallow. A hard-boiled egg she'd squandered a few precious cents on and had eaten on a park bench was more satisfying than the best cut of beef at Mrs. Campbell's table.

By the end of the week Mr. Roberts had made a place for her in the office as a clerk. Her wages to start would be five dollars a week. Mr. Roberts even advanced her the first week's pay. Rose was elated. Once again she had willed something and it had come true.

When she hurried home that afternoon, eager to tell Mrs. Campbell the happy news, Mr. Campbell let her in and said there was a letter waiting for her. It was propped on the hall table. It was from Mama.

Rose, dearest,

Mrs. Campbell has written to us about your predicament. Papa and I are heartsick for you, and I wonder that we ever let you go all alone. You have a good home to come back to, and don't worry about the money. We will manage, as we always have. We won't say a word. Just you come right away.

Your loving mother,
Mama Bess

Rose seethed. What right had that Mrs. Campbell to worry Mama, for no good reason at all? But her anger when she read Mama's letter was also strangely a relief. Rose lost the need to feel gratitude toward Mrs. Campbell any longer.

She could get along all right by herself, and she sat right down and wrote Mama that she could. She had a job at last. She did not mention the wages; she wrote only that she had a job and Mama and Papa were not to worry. She would be making more money soon and could send some home.

When she finished the letter, she put on it the last two-cent stamp she had left from the ones she'd brought with her from Mansfield. She hurried to drop it in the corner mailbox. Running back to the house, she met Mrs. Campbell returning from a sewing-circle meeting, neatly hatted and gloved. The expression in her pale-blue eyes behind the dotted veil suddenly made Rose see how disheveled she must look, bareheaded, her loosened hair ruffled by the breeze, her blouse sagging under her arms.

She stood awkwardly self-conscious while Mrs. Campbell unlocked the front door.

"Did you get your mother's letter?"

"Yes. I got it."

"Well, what did she say?"

Rose did not answer that. "I've a job," she said instead. Her breath came quickly.

"You do? What kind of job?"

Rose told her. They were in the hall now,

standing by the golden-oak hat tree at the foot of the stairs. The children watched from the parlor door.

Confusion and disapproval struggled on Mrs. Campbell's face.

"You think you're going to live in Kansas City on five dollars a week?"

"I'm going to. I've got to. I'll manage somehow," Rose said, a bit more defiantly than she wanted. Mrs. Campbell seemed to be eyeing her the way a cat does a cornered mouse.

"Oh, I don't doubt you'll manage!" Mrs. Campbell said cuttingly. She sailed down the hall. The slam of the kitchen door announced that she washed her hands of the whole affair.

But half an hour later Rose heard Mrs. Campbell's heavy footsteps coming up the stairs. Rose was sitting on the bed, her bag packed, trying to plan what to do. She had only the five dollars. It would be two weeks before she could get more money from the office.

Mrs. Campbell opened the door without knocking.

"I'm going to talk this over with you," she said firmly. "Don't you realize you can't get a decent room and anything to eat for five dollars a week? Do you think it's right to expect your folks to support you, poor as they are? It isn't—"

"I *don't* expect them to!" Rose declared. "It's just that—"

"—as though you didn't have a good home to go back to," Mrs. Campbell continued, letting Rose know that a well-bred girl ought not interrupt her elders. "Now be reasonable about this."

"I won't go back," Rose said flatly. Mrs. Campbell's expression reminded her of a horse with its ears laid back.

"Then you've decided, I suppose, where you are going?"

"No, I don't know. Can you tell me where to begin to look for a nice room that I can live in on my wages?"

"Oh, *really*!" Mrs. Campbell exclaimed

impatiently. Her voice grew colder while she continued to talk. Her arguments, her attempts at persuasion were of no use. Rose would not go home. She meant to keep her job and try to live on her wages.

"Well, then I guess you'll have to stay here," Mrs. Campbell said with a sigh. "I can't turn you out on the streets."

"How much would you charge for this room?" said Rose suddenly.

"Charge?" Mrs. Campbell said in surprise.

"I couldn't stay unless I paid you something. I'd have to do that."

"Well, of all the ungrateful . . ."

Tears came into Rose's eyes. She knew Mrs. Campbell meant well, and though she did not like her, she tried to thank her. But she did not know how to do it without giving in. She could only repeat that she must pay for the room.

"You are very kind, Mrs. Campbell," Rose kept saying. "But it wouldn't be right of me to take charity when I am perfectly able to pay my way."

Rose was shaken, but she felt a sense of victory in Mrs. Campbell's resigned attitude as she left the room.

Mrs. Campbell had finally agreed that Rose would pay five dollars a month for the room. But Rose's discomfort at having to live in that house, as kind as Mrs. Campbell meant to be, did not go away.

She tried to make as little trouble as possible. She made her bed neatly each morning and slipped out early so she would not meet any of the family. She spent her evenings after her work was done going to the library, where she could forget herself in books and in writing long letters to Paul, Aunt Eliza, Grandmother Wilder, Grandmother Ingalls and Aunt Mary, and of course, Mama and Papa.

She put as good a face on things as she could, the best face for Grandmother Wilder and Aunt Mary, and a little more honest in her letters to Aunt Eliza in Louisiana. She didn't want to worry anyone, but she did admit to

Aunt Eliza that life as a bachelor girl was harder than she expected.

"Every life is difficult," Aunt Eliza wrote back. "Were it not for eternal hope that things will improve, the human race would not exist."

It was only at the office that Rose could breathe freely. She worked from eight in the morning to six at night, taking only a short break for her midday meal, which, often as not, was a hard-boiled egg and some crackers or bread. From six at night until the office closed at nine o'clock, she stayed to practice on the telegraph instrument behind the tables where the real wires came in.

She worked hard at it, for at last she was on the road to the little station where she would work with Paul. Mr. Roberts was very kind. Often he came behind the screen where she was studying and talked to her for a long time. He was surprised at first by her working so hard. He seemed to think she had not been serious about it.

But his manner was so warm and friendly

that she told him about everything, except
Paul.

Rose told him about Mr. Weeks and that she
did not know what she would have done if
she had not gotten the job. She was very grateful to Mr. Roberts and tried to tell him so.

Some days he gave her a great deal of work
to do and was cross when she made mistakes.
She did her best, trying hard to please him,
and he was soon friendly again.

His was the only friendliness she found to
warm her shivering spirit. Rose was puzzled
by his affectionate interest in her and his sudden coldness when she eagerly thanked him.
But this was only part of the bewildering world
of the office. She felt many hidden currents
that she could not understand.

Mr. McCormick, the young operator with
the green eyeshade, for instance, always re-
garded her with a weary, slightly amused eye.
He seemed to be sitting in judgment of her
and expecting her to fail. She wouldn't fail,
of course. She was getting better, faster, every
day.

She decided that too much looking at life from the back-door keyhole of the telegraph operator's point of view had made him too worldly-wise for his own good.

When he was on duty in the long, slow evenings, Rose, practicing diligently behind her screen, heard him singing a popular song thoughtfully:

"Life's a funny proposition after all;
just why we're here and what it's all about.
It's a problem that has driven many brainy
*   men to drink,*
It's a problem that they've never figured out."

Life seemed simple enough to Rose. She would be a full-fledged telegraph operator soon, earning as much as fifty dollars a month. She could begin to repay Mama and Papa the hundred dollars then, buy some new clothes, and have plenty to eat.

She would try to get a job at the Sacramento station. Always in the back of her mind was the thought of Paul. She occupied her mind with plans for the furnishing of housekeeping rooms, and ideas for making curtains and embroidering napkins. Those thoughts filled her with hope and helped cleanse her of the discouraging mood around her.

A Real Celebration

The days turned into weeks, then the weeks flowed into months. Mr. Roberts promoted Rose to operator, but she received no increase in her pay.

Before she knew it, her eighteenth birthday—December fifth—came and went. She spent it working. That night she sat alone in her room reading the letters and cards she had received from her family and from Paul.

Mama had sent a beautiful burgundy and pale-yellow bear's claw quilt she and some of her women friends had been sewing on since the summer. It was lovely and smelled freshly laundered. But it only made Rose feel more lonely, cut off from everything she had ever known. And it reminded her of how far she had to go before she and Paul could marry. She dreamed of the day they would have a little house of their own, with the quilt to brighten it up and remind her of Mama.

Christmas was even worse. Mr. Roberts pinned a dusty wreath on the office door. Rose would have to work on the holiday, as she was the newest operator. She didn't have the money to travel even if she could have.

She had knitted good wool socks for Papa and made up a pair of lace handkerchiefs for Mama. Her eyes brimmed with unshed tears when she handed the little wrapped package to the clerk at the post office, thinking of Mama and Papa alone on Christmas for the second year in a row.

It was a burden of sorts, she thought, to be an only child. If she had had brothers and sisters, her guilt would not have been so keen.

She sent Paul a copy of a book by an adventure writer, Jack London, called *The Sea-Wolf*. She was lucky to find a used copy. Mr. London was also a socialist, and Rose had read his latest book, *War of the Classes*, which she thought was very radical in the way he predicted a real war between the working class and the ruling class.

Revolution was happening everywhere in the world, it seemed. Rose had kept her appetite for the newspapers and read every one that customers left in the telegraph office. She read about miners striking in Colorado, Bolsheviks in Russia—the world was brimming with the romance and tragedy of struggle and change.

Rose realized how far she had drifted since the past winter, when she had helped her aunt Eliza in Louisiana handing out pamphlets for the socialist cause and met Mr. Debs. She felt badly that she wasn't doing something to further the cause, but her heart just wasn't in it anymore.

In the days leading up to Christmas, Rose

sent out messages of cheer and good wishes for customers who also were far from their families. She shared secretly in their loneliness and drew a little strength from knowing she was not the only one separated from home and loved ones.

It was early spring when Paul finally wrote that he was coming to spend a day in Kansas City. He was going to Mansfield to help his mother move to Sacramento to live with him. On the way he would stop and see Rose.

Rose, in happy excitement, thought of her clothes. She must have something new to wear when they met. Paul must see in the first glance how much she had changed, how much she had improved. She had not been able to save anything yet. All her money went to her room and her food, and to Mama and Papa. But she must, *must* have new clothes.

Two days of worried planning brought her courage to the point of asking Mr. Roberts for her next two weeks' salary in advance. Her food was a problem she would try to meet later. Mr. Roberts was very kind about it.

"Money? Of course!" he said. He took a bill from his own pocketbook. "We'll have to see about your getting more money pretty soon." Her heart leaped at this promise of a raise.

She went out at noon and bought a white pleated voile skirt for five dollars, a China-silk shirtwaist for three ninety-five, and a white straw sailor hat for a dollar and a half. She asked for them to be delivered to the Campbells' house. And that afternoon Mr. McCormick, with his sneering smile, handed her a note that had come over the wire for her: "Arrive eight ten Sunday morning. Meet me. Paul."

She went back to her room that evening so confidently happy that she rang the doorbell without her usual qualm. Mrs. Campbell's lips were drawn into a tight, thin line.

"There are some packages for you," she said.

"Yes, I know. I bought some clothes. Thank you for taking them in," said Rose. She felt friendly even toward Mrs. Campbell. "A white voile skirt, and a silk waist, and a hat. Would you like to see them?"

"No, thank you!" said Mrs. Campbell icily. Going up the stairs, Rose heard her speaking to her husband. "'I bought some clothes,' she says, bold as brass. Clothes!"

The words cut Rose. She knew the clothes were an extravagance, but she did want them so badly, for Paul. How could people be so unkind? It seemed to her that she had worked hard enough to deserve them. Besides, hadn't Mr. Roberts said that she might get a raise?

She was dressed and creeping noiselessly out of the house by seven o'clock Sunday morning. The spring dawn was coming rosily into the city after a night of rain; the odor of the freshly washed lawns and flower beds was delicious, and birds sang in the trees.

The flavor of the cool, sweet air and the warmth of the sunshine mingled with her joyful sense of coming happiness. She looked very well, she thought, watching her slim white reflection in the shop windows.

When the train pulled into the big, dingy station, Rose had been waiting for some time, her pulses fluttering with excitement. But her self-confidence fled when she saw the crowds pouring from the cars. She shrank back into the waiting-room doorway; and she saw Paul before his eager eyes found her.

It was a shock to find that he had changed too. His self-confident walk, his prosperous appearance in a new suit gave her the chilly sensation that she was about to meet a stranger. She braced herself, but when they shook hands, she felt that hers was cold.

"You're looking well," she said shyly.

"Well, so are you," he answered. They walked down the platform together, and she saw that he carried a new suitcase, and that even his shoes were new and shining.

"Where shall we go?" They hesitated, looking at each other, and in their smiles the strangeness vanished.

"I don't care. Anywhere, if you're along," Paul said. "Oh, Rose, it sure is great to see you again! You look like a million dollars." His approving eye was upon her new clothes.

"I'm glad you think so," she said, radiant. "That's an awfully nice suit, Paul." Happiness came back to her in a flood. She put out her hand and picked a bit of thread from his sleeve. "Well, where shall we go?"

"We'll get something to eat first," he said. "I'm about starved, aren't you?" She had not thought of eating, but realized she was starving too.

They breakfasted in a little restaurant near the station on waffles and sausages and coffee. The hot food was delicious, and the waiter in the soiled white apron grinned understandingly while he served them. Paul gave him a dime in an offhand manner, and she thrilled at his careless extravagance and his air of knowing his way about.

The whole long day lay before them, bright with limitless possibilities. They left the suitcase with the cashier of the restaurant and walked slowly down the street.

Rose suggested that they walk awhile in the downtown, and perhaps in the afternoon enjoy a car ride to a new amusement park at the edge of the city.

"Nothing like that," Paul declared. "I want

a real celebration, a regular blowout. I've been saving up for it a long time. It won't do any harm to miss church one Sunday. Let's take a boat down the Missouri River."

"Oh, Paul!" Rose was dazzled. "But won't it be awfully expensive?"

"I don't care how much it costs," he replied. "Come on. It'll be fun."

They went down the shabby streets toward the river, and even the dingy tenements and broken sidewalks of the waterfront quarter, where many immigrants lived, seemed to have a holiday air.

They laughed about the strange little shops and the restaurant windows where electric lights burned in the clear daylight over tired-looking pies and cakes.

It was like going into a foreign land together, she said. Even Paul was touched by the enchantment she saw in it all, though he did not conceal his disapproval of these foreigners.

"We're going to see to it we don't have too many of them in Sacramento," he said.

Already there were too many Chinese immigrants, he explained, as well as Hindus and Japanese, and who knew what else.

Rose didn't like to hear Paul talk that way. She knew from the newspapers that many Americans were unhappy about the large numbers of people who had recently immigrated. She also knew that every single American was an immigrant at one time. The country was built by immigrants. She had no quarrel with immigrants, but she didn't want to spoil Paul's good mood, so she kept her thoughts to herself.

"Now this is more like it!" Paul exclaimed when he had helped Rose along the gangplank and gotten her safely on the deck of the steamer. Rose, pressing his arm with her fingers, was too happy to speak.

The boat was filling with people in Sunday clothes. Everywhere about them was the exciting stir of departure, calls, commands, the thump of boxes being loaded on the deck below. A whistle sounded hoarsely; the engines were starting, sending a thrill through the very planks beneath their feet.

"We'd better get a good place up in front," said Paul. He took her through the magnificence of a large room furnished with velvet chairs, past a glimpse of shining white tables and white-clad waiters. They found a seat from which they could gaze down at the great muddy river.

"Remember all those years back, when our families were traveling in wagons from South Dakota?" Paul recalled. "We crossed the Missouri at Yankton. It's hard to imagine now. I was just a ten-year-old, driving a big wagon and team."

Rose admired Paul's ease and assurance. She looked at him with an admiration that she would not allow to lessen even when the boat edged out into the stream and, turning, revealed that he had led her by mistake to the stern deck.

She suggested they explore the boat, to help Paul conceal his embarrassment. She listened, enthralled by his explanations of all they saw.

He estimated the price of the crates of vegetables and chickens piled on the lower deck. His description of the engines caught the attention of a grimy engineer, who had emerged from the noisy depths for a breath of air. The engineer, with a friendly gaze, offered to show them the engine room.

Rose could not understand his explanations, but she was interested because Paul was. She was charmed to discover a dim tank half filled with flopping fish that had been scooped from the river and flung there by the paddle wheel.

"We take 'em home and eat 'em, miss," said the engineer.

When they returned again to the upper decks, she was disappointed to find that they could see nothing but green levee banks on either side of the river. The banks were so high, they couldn't see the land beyond.

But Paul noticed a slender iron ladder that led to another deck. He climbed it, helping Rose up after him. There they could see beyond the levee an astounding stretch of water where land should be.

Their amazement emboldened Paul to tap on the glass wall of a small room beside them, in which an old man sat peacefully smoking his pipe. He was the pilot, who explained that it was floodwater they saw.

He let them squeeze into his tiny quarters and stay while he told long stories of early days on the river, of floods in which whole settlements were swept away at night, of women and children rescued from floating roofs, of cows found drowned in treetops, and droves of hogs that cut their own throats with their hoofs while swimming.

Listening to him while the boat slowly chugged around the curves of the sunlit river, Rose felt the romance of living, the color of all the millions of unsung lives in the world.

"Isn't everything interesting!" she cried, giving Paul's arm an excited squeeze as they walked along the main deck again. "Oh, I'd like to live all the lives that ever were lived! Think of those women and the miners and people in cities and everything!"

"I expect you'd find it mighty inconvenient before you got through," Paul said. Then he added, "Gee, you're awfully pretty, Rose," and they forgot everything except that they were together.

If I Had a Little Money

They had to get off at Lexington in order to catch the late-afternoon boat back to Kansas City. There was just time to eat on board, Paul said, and waving aside her protests, he led her into the white-painted dining room.

The smooth linen, the shining silver, and the imposing waiters confused her; she was able to see nothing but the prices on the fancy menu cards, and they were terrifying. Paul himself was startled by them, and she could see worried calculation in his eyes.

She wished Paul would let her pay her share; she was working, too, and earning money. The memories of the advance she had drawn on her wages, and her uncomfortable life in Mrs. Campbell's house, passed through her mind like a shadow. But they were gone in an instant, and she sat happily at the white table, eating small delicious sandwiches and drinking milk, smiling across immaculate linen at Paul.

For a moment she played with the fancy that this was a honeymoon trip, and a thrill ran along her nerves.

They were at Lexington before they knew it. There was a moment of flurried haste, and then they were standing on the levee, watching the boat push off and disappear beyond a wall of willow trees. A few loungers looked at them with expressionless eyes. Rose and Paul heard that the afternoon boat was late, and it might be along about five o'clock.

"Well, that'll still get us back in time for my train," Paul said. "Let's look around a little."

The road that ran along the top of the levee was a tunnel of budding willow boughs. The ground was covered with soft sand in which their feet made no sound. They walked in an enchanted stillness, through pale light, green as seawater, drowsy, warm, and scented with the breath of unseen flowers.

They caught glimpses of the broad yellow river through the branches. The waves of the river gave back the color of the sky in flashes of metallic blue. Suddenly, stepping out of the shadows, they saw a mass of flowers. A sea of petals, unearthly as waves of pure rosy light, rippled at their feet.

The loveliness of it filled Rose's eyes with tears. "Oh!" she said, softly. "Oh, Paul!" Her hand went out blindly toward him. One more breath of magic would make the moment perfect.

She did not know what she wanted, but her whole being longed for it. "Oh, Paul!"

"Pears. Hundreds of acres, Rose," he cried. "They're the tops of trees! We're looking down at 'em! Look at the river. Why, the land's

fifteen feet below water level. Did you ever see anything like it?"

Excitement shook his voice. "There must be a way to get down there. I want to see it!" He almost ran along the edge of the levee; Rose had to hurry to keep beside him. She did not know why she should be hurt because Paul was interested in the orchards. She tried to cover her disappointment by being the first to laugh about going downstairs to farm when they found the wooden steps on the side of the levee.

She half listened to Paul's talk about irrigation and the soil. He crumbled handfuls of it between his fingers while they walked between the orchard rows.

It came to her suddenly to wonder about the girls in Sacramento. There must be some, but Paul had never written about them. She thought about it for some time before she could find the courage to ask about them.

"Girls?" Paul said. "Sure there are. I don't pay much attention to them, though. I see them in church, and they're at the Aid Society suppers, of course. They seem pretty foolish to me.

"Why, I never noticed whether they were pretty or not." Then his face brightened. "I'll tell you; they don't seem to talk about anything much. You're the only girl I ever knew who I could really talk to. I've been awfully lonesome, thinking about you."

"Really truly?" she said, looking up at him. The sunlight fell across her white dress, and stray pink petals fluttered slowly down around her. "Have you really been lonesome for me too?" She swayed toward him, ever so little, and he put his arms around her.

He did love her, Rose saw. A great contentment flowed through her. To be in his arms again was to be safe and rested and warm after what had seemed ages of struggling in the cold.

He was thinking only of her now. His arms held her against him; she felt the roughness of his coat under her cheek. He was stammering words of love, kissing her hair.

"Oh, Paul, I love you, I love you, I love

you!" she said, her arms around his neck.

They found a little nook under the willows on the levee bank and sat there with the river rippling at their feet, his arm around her, her head on his shoulder.

They talked a little then. Paul told her again all about Sacramento, but she did not mind. "When we're married . . ." said Paul, and the rest of the sentence did not matter.

"And I'm going to help you," Rose said. "Because I'm telegraphing now too. I'll be earning as much . . . almost as much as you do. We can live over the depot."

"We will not!" said Paul. "We'll have a house. Anyhow, I don't know that I'm crazy about my wife working."

"Oh, but I do want to help! And a house would be nice. Oh, Paul, with rosebushes in the yard!"

"And a horse and buggy, so we can go riding Sunday afternoons."

"Besides, if I'm making money . . ." Rose said.

"I know. We wouldn't have to wait so long.

Of course there's Mother. And I want to feel that I can support . . ."

Rose felt the magic fading.

"Never mind!" he declared. The tiniest of cuddling movements brought his arms tight around her again.

They were startled when they noticed the shadows under the trees. They had not dreamed it was so late. They raced for the landing. The river was an empty stretch of dirty gray lapping dusky banks. There was no one at the landing.

"It must be way after five o'clock," Paul said worriedly. "I wish I had my watch. But the boat couldn't have gone by without our seeing it!" The mere possibility drained the color from their cheeks. They looked at each other with wide eyes. "It couldn't have possibly! Let's ask."

The little town was no more than half a dozen old wooden buildings facing the levee. A store, unlighted and locked, a harness shop, also locked, two dark warehouses, a saloon. Rose waited in the shadow of it while Paul went in to inquire. He came out almost immediately.

"No, the boat hasn't gone. They don't know when it'll get here."

They walked with uncertainty back to the landing and stood gazing at the darkening river. "I suppose there's no knowing when it will get here?" Rose said. "There's no other way of getting back?"

"No, there's no railroad. I have got you into a scrape!"

"It's all right. It wasn't your fault," Rose hastened to say. They walked up and down, waiting. Darkness came. The river breeze grew colder. Stars appeared.

"Chilly?" he asked

"A little," she said through chattering teeth. He took off his coat and wrapped it around her, despite her protests. They found a sheltered place on the bank and huddled together, shivering. A delicious sleepiness stole over her, and the lap-lap of the water, the whispering of the leaves, the warmth of Paul's shoulder under her cheek—all became like a dream.

If I Had a Little Money

"Comfortable, dear?"

"Mmmmmhuh," she murmured. "You?"

"You bet your life!" She roused a little to meet his kiss. The night became dreamlike again.

"Rose?"

"What?"

"Seems to me we've been here a long time. What'll we do? We can't stay here till morning."

"I don't know why not," she said. "All night under the stars . . ."

"But listen. What if the boat comes by and doesn't stop? There isn't any light."

She sat up then, rubbing the drowsiness from her eyes.

"Well, let's make a fire. Got any matches?"

He always carried them, to light the railroad switch lamps in Sacramento. They hunted dry branches and driftwood and coaxed a flickering blaze alive.

"It's like being stranded on a desert island!" She laughed. His eyes adored her as she crouched with disheveled hair in the leaping yellow light.

"You're certainly game," he said. "I think you're the pluckiest girl in the world. And when I think what a fool I was to get you into this!"

Like an echo down the river came the hoarse whistle of the boat. A moment later it was upon them, looming white and gigantic, its lights cutting swaths in the darkness as it edged in to the landing.

Struggling to straighten her hat, to tuck up her hair, to brush the sand from her skirt, Rose stumbled aboard with Paul's hand steadying her.

The blaze of the salon lights hurt their eyes, but warmth and security relaxed their tired muscles. The room was empty, its carpet swept, the velvet chairs neatly in place.

"Funny, I thought there'd be a lot of passengers," Paul wondered aloud. He found a cushion, tucked it behind Rose's head, and sat down beside her. "Well, we're all right now. We'll be in Kansas City pretty soon."

"Don't let's think about it," she said with quivering lips. "I hate to have it all end, such a lovely day. It'll be such a long time before we have another."

Paul held her hand tightly. "Not so awfully long," he promised. "I'm not going to stand for it." He spoke firmly, but his eyes were troubled. She did not answer, and they sat, each thinking about the future, while the boat jolted on toward the moment of their parting.

"Damn being poor!" Paul suddenly spat out. The word startled Rose. Paul so sincerely and humbly a church member—swearing! He went on without a pause. "If I had a little money, if I only had a little money! What right has it got to make such a difference? Oh, Rose, you don't know how I wish we could be married right today!"

"Paul, Paul dear, you mustn't!" She drew his dear, tousled head against her shoulder.

After a moment he pushed away from her and got up.

"I seem to be making a fool of myself generally," he said shakily. He walked about the room, looking with an appearance of interest at the pictures on the walls.

"It's funny there aren't more people on board," he said after a while. "Well, I guess I'll go see what time we get in." He came back five minutes later, an odd expression on his face.

"Look, Rose," he said gruffly. "We won't get in for hours. Something wrong with the engines. They're only making half time. I don't know why I didn't think of it before. You've got to work tomorrow and all. The man suggested . . ." Paul paused.

"Well, for goodness' sake, suggested what?"

"Everybody else has berths," he said. "You'd better let me get you one, because there's no sense in your sitting up all night. There's no knowing when we'll get in."

A vision of the office went through Rose's mind, and she saw herself, sleepy eyed, struggling to get messages into the right envelopes and trying to manage the unruly messenger boys. She was tired. But a berth would be awfully expensive, no doubt.

"But Paul, I hate to have you spend so much. I could sleep a little right here. And besides, I'd rather stay here with you," she said.

"So would I. But we might as well be sensible. You've got to work, and I'd probably go to sleep, too. Come on, let's see how much it is, anyhow."

They found the right place after wandering twice around the boat. A weary man sat behind the half door, adding up a column of figures.

"Berths? Sure. Outside, of course. One left. Dollar and a half." Paul pulled the money from his pocket without a moment's hesitation. Rose thought it was wonderful that Paul was so good to her, but she shuddered to think of the cost, just for a few hours' sleep.

The man came out of his office, yawning, a key with a dangling tag in his hand. "This way."

They followed him down the corridor. Matters seemed to be taken from their hands. He stepped out on the dark deck.

"Careful there, better give your wife a hand over those ropes," he cautioned over his shoulder, and they heard the sound of a key in a lock. Rose felt herself blush in the dark.

An oblong of light appeared; he stepped aside again to let them pass him. They went in.

"There's towels. Everything all right, I guess," he said cheerfully. "Good night."

Rose met Paul's eyes and they stared at each other for one horrified second. Then, suddenly, Rose began to giggle, a combination of happiness and nervousness. Paul looked at her strangely for a moment. Then he started to laugh as well. As embarrassing as it was to be taken for a married couple, it seemed to make the possibility of being together forever more real.

"I guess I better go now," Paul finally said. He fumbled with the door. "Good night."

"Good night." Rose felt suddenly forlorn. But he was not gone.

"Rose? We could be married—we could be, if you wanted—just as soon as we get to

Kansas City. The very first thing in the morning! We could manage somehow."

"We can't," Rose said soberly. "I'd be spoiling everything for you. Your mother and me and everything on your hands and you're just getting started. You'd hate me after a while. No, no, no!"

"I could never hate you, Rose. Oh, what am I saying?" he added hoarsely. Rose turned away from him, hiding her face.

Paul stumbled, stepping over the sill. A rush of cold moist air blew in upon her from the open doorway. He was gone. She got the door shut and sat down on the edge of the berth. A cool breeze flowed in like water through the shutters of the windows; she felt the throbbing of the engines.

She could not bear the light even through her closed lids, and after a while she turned it out and lay open eyed in the darkness thinking and wondering.

She had drifted off into a troubled sleep when the stopping of the boat struck her aching nerves. She sat up, feeling groggy, pushing her hair back from a face that felt lumpy and lifeless. The pale dawn filled the cabin. She smoothed her hair, straightened her crumpled dress as well as she could, and went out on the deck. The boat lay at the Kansas City landing.

A few feet away Paul was leaning upon the railing, his face white and drawn in the cold light. She made herself smile, to make him feel better. "We'd better be getting off, hadn't we?"

Paul took Rose's arm and guided her down the gangplank onto the dock. Fuzzy from lack of sleep, she felt as though she was floating in a dream.

The grayness of dawn was in the air. A few workmen plodded past them, carrying lunch pails and tools. A baker's wagon rattled by, making loud echoes.

Paul would not stop criticizing himself. Rose tried to comfort him, but he kept coming up with another thing to fret about.

"I hope you don't get into a row with the folks you're staying with. If you do, Rose, you must let me know. I wouldn't stand for anything like that."

He told Rose she could reach him in Mansfield until he came back again on his way home. He hadn't thought he could stop on the way, but he would. He'd be worried about her until he saw her again and was sure everything was all right. He had been an awful boob to take a chance on taking the boat. He'd never forgive himself if . . .

Rose turned to peer after a young man who had passed them in the street and smiled at her. The motion was almost automatic; she had hardly seen the man, and not until he was past did her tired mind recall his cynical smile.

"What is it?" Paul broke off in the middle of his talking.

"Nothing," she said. It had been Mr. McCormick, from the office. But it would require too much effort to talk about him. As dulled as she was from lack of sleep, she felt her heart skip a beat. What would it mean, Mr. McCormick seeing her in such a state?

The blinds of Mrs. Campbell's house were still down when they reached it. The tightly rolled morning paper lay on the porch. She and Paul faced each other on the damp cement walk, the freshness of the dewy lawns about them.

"Well, good-bye."

"Good-bye."

They felt shy in the daylight, under the blank stare of the windows. Their hands clung.

"You'll let me know if—if there's any trouble?"

She promised, though she had no intention of bothering him with her problems. It was not his fault that the boat was late, and she had gone as gladly as he.

"Don't worry about it; I'll be all right. Good-bye, Paul."

"Good-bye, Rose." Still their fingers clung together. She felt a rush of tenderness toward him.

"Don't look so worried, dear!" Quickly, daringly, she leaned toward him and brushed a butterfly's wing of a kiss upon his cheek.

Then she ran up the steps and rang the bell.
There was time for the momentary glow to
depart, leaving her weak and chilly, before
Mrs. Campbell opened the door.

She said nothing. Her eyes, her tight lips,
her manner of drawing her dressing gown back
from Rose's approach spoke her thoughts. No
amount of explaining would ever convince
Mrs. Campbell to believe Rose's innocent
story of the slow boat.

So Rose held her head high and countered
silence with silence. But before she reached
her room, she heard Mrs. Campbell's voice,
high-pitched, speaking to her husband.

"That's what I get for taking her in out of
charity! The only thing to do is to put her out
of this house before we have a scandal on our
hands."

Rose shut her door softly. She would
leave the house that very day. The battered
alarm clock pointed to half past five. Three
hours before she must be at work. She undressed mechanically, half-formed plans rushing through her mind.

She had no money, having spent her next two weeks' wages for these crumpled clothes. She could telegraph Mama and Papa, but she must not alarm them.

There was Mr. Roberts, but she could never catch up with all she owed. Perhaps he would advance the raise he had promised.

Her brain worked with hectic speed. She saw in flashes rooming houses, the office, Mr. Roberts, Mr. McCormick. She thought out every detail of long conversations, heard her own voice explaining, arguing, promising, thanking.

She lay down on her bed, trying to figure out what to do next.

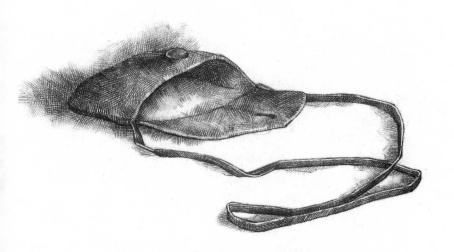

Call Me Miss Wilder

Rose awoke with a start at the sound of the alarm. Her brief sleep had not refreshed her. Her body felt wooden, and her eyes felt like they had grit in them.

Dressing and hurrying to the office was like a nightmare in which every movement took the greatest effort and accomplished nothing. But the office routine helped her catch her balance.

She booked the night messages, laying wet tissue paper over them, running them through the machine that made a copy onto the tissue, addressing their envelopes, sending out messenger boys, settling their disputes over long routes. Everything was as usual. The sunshine streamed in through the plate-glass front of the office. Customers came and went. The telephone rang. The instruments clicked.

Her holiday was gone as if she had dreamed it. There remained only the remembered sting of Mrs. Campbell's expression, and a determination to leave that house.

Rose tried several times to speak with Mr. Roberts. But he was in a black mood. He walked past her without saying good morning, and over the matter of a delayed message his voice snapped like a whiplash.

Perhaps he would be in a better humor later. She must ask him for some money before night.

Among the stacks of incoming messages there were often notices of jobs for operators in other parts of the country. She stuffed one notice from Western Union in San Francisco into the pile of delivered wires. They needed a night operator at the St. Francis Hotel and would pay forty-five dollars a month.

So much money, she thought. It didn't seem fair, her slaving away for just a few dollars. She sighed and buried herself in the flow of work.

In the lull just before noon she sat at her table behind the screen, her head on her arms. She did not feel like working at the instrument.

Mr. McCormick was lounging against the front counter, talking to Mr. Roberts, who sat at his desk. They would take care of any customers; for a moment she could rest and try to think.

Finally she gathered her wits and her courage. She got to her feet, groggy with having nearly fallen asleep. Mr. Roberts laughed at something Mr. McCormick had said.

"Mr. Roberts," she began, "I would like to speak to you about my pay."

Mr. McCormick went to his desk and began sending out wires.

"What of it?" Mr. Roberts answered.

"Didn't I tell you we'd see about getting you some more money?"

"Yes," Rose said, wavering a moment in her resolve. She hated to sound greedy or nagging. But she had no choice. Her back was to the wall.

"Well," Mr. Roberts said, putting his hands on his hips, "then the matter is closed."

"But I can't live anymore on what you're paying me!" Rose heard the pleading in her voice, and panic rising in her chest. She tried to stifle the feeling, but she was tired and feeling desperate. "Why, I'll just bet you're paying Mr. McCormick many times what you're paying me, and I—"

"Don't you tell me what I'm paying anybody," Mr. Roberts interrupted, his face darkening with anger. "You are a long way, young lady, from achieving the speed and accuracy of any man I've ever had in any office I've ever managed. Furthermore, perhaps if you weren't out gadding about till all hours, as I've just been told you did last night, you might find you have the money to live on without robbing from Peter to pay Paul. I should say that in my day . . ."

Rose could not bear to hear another word. Tears flooded her eyes. She turned and fled to the back of the office. Through her blurred vision she found the rickety stairway that led down into the basement.

She slumped down onto an old crate by the shelves of batteries that ran the telegraph keys, turned against the cobwebbed boards, and wept. She hated herself for doing it, but she could not help herself. She kept trying to stop, and soon she was able to do so.

She waited awhile among the uncaring battery jars, steadying herself and wiping her face with her handkerchief. When she forced herself to climb up into the daylight again, Mr. Roberts was gone.

Mr. McCormick sat at the San Francisco wire, gazing into space, whistling the tune "Life's a Funny Proposition After All."

The sounder clattered fretfully, calling him. But he had turned a deaf ear.

Rose knew she must leave the office at

once. She put on her hat and marched out the door, slamming it a little louder than she'd meant.

When she was out in the harsh sunlight, with the eyes of passersby upon her, she squirmed among her prickly thoughts. The side streets were better than the others—fewer people could see her. If only it were night, so she could crawl into some corner and die.

It was a long time before Rose realized that her body was aching and her feet hurt from walking. How far had she gone? She had reached a street in some residential subdivision, where cement sidewalks ran through tangles of last year's weeds. Little cottages stood forlornly at long intervals.

She stumbled over a vacant lot of dry stubble and weeds and sat down on a discarded crate. It was good to sit outside and be alone.

For the first time Rose thought her life was a failure. She had been so disappointed that she no longer felt the pain, but her soul was still tortured.

There was no refuge and no time to heal

her hurt soul. There was no one to help her bear it. For the first time, Rose felt worse than lonely. She was *alone*.

The afternoon was almost gone. At the house there was Mrs. Campbell. At the office . . . She shivered when her thoughts touched Paul. She couldn't tell him what had happened.

She could get what she owed Mr. Roberts from Mama and Papa and go home to stay. She still owed them eighty dollars, months of small sacrifices and heartbreaking work. Somehow she must find strength in herself to stand up, to go on, to do *something*.

But before she could get another telegraph job, she would need a recommendation from Mr. Roberts. Telegraphing was all she knew how to do.

In the depth of her mind Rose felt a hardness growing. All the lessons of her upbringing, the gentleness and the fairness and the civility, had not helped her. Something else was needed. She lifted her chin, set her lips, and narrowed her eyes in thought.

After a long time she stood, brushing dead

grass stalks from her skirt, and started back to town. A streetcar came along, and she was so tired that she took it despite the cost.

On the way she remembered that she should eat, and she thought of Mrs. Brown. Her last half-punched meal ticket was still in her purse. She had never wanted to see Mrs. Brown again. Many times she had thought to throw away the ticket, but she had not been able to do so because it represented food.

But when she got off the car at the corner nearest the little restaurant and forced herself to walk up to its doors, she found it closed and empty. A FOR RENT sign was glued to the grimy window.

Rose felt a moment of relief. She hadn't really wanted to see Mrs. Brown. But then she felt a pang of sorrow and pity. Mrs. Brown had failed. Rose was in danger of failing too.

In a dairy lunchroom she drank a cup of coffee and swallowed a sandwich. She used all but the last pennies to her name. It was almost as if she had to go right down to nothing before she would have the courage to start back up again.

Then she went back to the telegraph office.

She held her head high and walked as if going to her own execution. She felt she had to harden herself before she could make herself face Mr. Roberts again.

She opened the office door and went in. Mr. Roberts was at one of the wires. Mr. McCormick, frowning, was booking messages at her high desk. She hung her hat in the cabinet and took the pen from his hand and a message from the pile.

"Well, Miss Bright Eyes, welcome to our city!" he exclaimed in his usual manner. But she saw that he was nervous, agitated by the tension in the air.

"After this you'll call me Miss Wilder," she declared, folding a message into an envelope. She struck the bell for the next messenger boy.

Well, she had been able to do that.

It was harder to approach Mr. Roberts. Rose did not know whether she despised him or feared him, but she felt ill when he came through the railing into the office and sat down at his desk.

She went over the day's bookings and checked the messenger books without seeing them, until her courage began to win in its battle over her cowardice.

Then she went over to his desk.

"Mr. Roberts," she said clearly. "I'm not as good as Mr. McCormick. I know that." Her cheeks, her forehead, even her neck were burning painfully. "But it isn't right, your paying me so much less than other operators earn. I work hard and am always here on time and always get my work done."

"Well, there's no use making such a fuss about it," he mumbled, searching among his papers for one that apparently was not there.

"I wouldn't stay," Rose went on. "Only I owe you ten dollars and I've got to have a job. You know that. I've got to stay here—"

"How do you know I'm going to let you?" he interrupted, still not looking at her.

Rose hesitated, thrown off guard. "I'm a good clerk. You can't get another as good any cheaper. You ought to anyway let me keep the job, at least so I can pay back—"

"That'll do," he said harshly. Turning away from her, he caught Mr. McCormick's eye, which dropped quickly to the message he was sending.

Rose had to face the crisis. Her mind whirled. Dared she . . . ?

She walked woodenly back to her desk and shuffled the papers until she found the all-stations message that had come in the morning.

Then she sat down and scribbled on a blank message form with her pencil:

> *Can arrive in two days*
> *for permanent duty*
> *Calvin Roberts will confirm*
> *experience at Kansas City office*

Her hand steely, her mind shaking, Rose walked to Mr. Roberts' desk and dropped both messages on it. She wanted to ask him, "Shall I send it?" But the words clogged together in her throat.

Mr. Roberts read them twice and stared at the wall. He handed them back without looking at her and said sarcastically, "I'll try to keep the office going without your assistance."

She had won. Hers was the next wire out. Mr. McCormick saw it and grinned. It startled her to find a little twisted smile forming itself on her own lips.

In the middle of the afternoon she was leaning on the front counter, watching people go by outside the plate-glass windows. She was wondering what was the truth about them, whether they were happy with their lives, whether they were loved, if their dreams were coming true or not, when she felt Mr. McCormick's gaze upon her.

He put his elbow on the counter beside hers and spoke confidentially. "Bryant at San Francisco just wired. You're to go straight to the office when you get off the ferry that connects with the train at Oakland. You know, you're darn plucky. I like you."

Rose said nothing, privately enjoying a moment of victory. They avoided each other's gaze.

"By the way," he said, as if suddenly remembering something, "I made a killing at poker last night."

When Rose stared blankly at him, he added, "There's no string tied to a little loan."

"Yes. I suppose. I'll go now," she said, exhausted of feeling. "I think everything's in order. The Ramsey message was sent out twice."

Against her will, but with no other choice, she borrowed ten dollars from Mr. McCormick, promising to return it at the end of the month. He kissed the money good-bye in a grand gesture. She was too tired even to be offended.

She spent twenty-five cents of it to send a message from the train depot to Paul, even though Mr. McCormick would have sent it for her at no cost. She didn't want him to know a thing more about her, or to have a thing more to do with him. She wished she could take a long, hot bath and cleanse herself of Kansas City.

The Big City

Cooped up in a narrow space at the end of a long corridor, Rose sat at her desk gazing in awe at the life of a great San Francisco hotel, the St. Francis. Every moment the color and glitter shifted under the brilliant light of mammoth chandeliers.

Tall, gilded elevator doors opened and closed. Women passed, wrapped in satins and velvets, airy feathers in their shining hair. Men in evening dress escorted them. Bellboys in tight-waisted uniforms walked briskly by, carrying silver trays and announcing names she couldn't understand. Their high voices rose above the constant muffled stir and the faint sounds of music from a band that was playing in the Blue Room.

Rose had choked the telegraph sounder with a pencil, to stop its chattering so that she might hear the music. But the tones of the violins came to her blurred by a low hum of voices, by the rustle of silks, by the soft movement of many feet on velvet carpets.

No sound was clear. Her ears were baffled, as her eyes were dazzled and her thoughts confused by all those sensations. San Francisco was a cyclone, an endless roaring circle, fantastic and dizzying.

This had been her impression of it on that first morning, when she struggled through the swirling crowds at the ferry building, lugging her telescope bag with one hand and with the other trying to hold her hat in place against gusts of wind.

Beneath the uproar of streetcar gongs, of huge wagons rumbling over the cobbles, of hundreds of hurrying feet, whistles, bells, shouts, she had felt a great current, terrifyingly careless of anything but its own mighty swirl.

Now, even after a month in San Francisco, her impression was the same. But Rose seemed to have been drawn into the center of the cyclone. The city roared around her, still confusing, still driven by its own breathless speed, but in the heart of it she was untouched. She had found nothing for herself in all that motion and sound.

Her first fears of the big city had vanished. She had gathered her strength for a great effort, and she had found nothing to do. Far from lying in wait with nameless dangers for the innocent stranger, the city did not even know she was there.

At the main Western Union office, Mr. Bryant had received her with indifference. He was a busy man. She was just one small detail of his routine work.

He sent her to the St. Francis Hotel, asking her to report there at five o'clock in the afternoon and, looking at her again, asking whether she knew anyone in San Francisco or had arranged for a place to live. Three minutes later he handed her over to a brisk young woman, who gave her an address and told her what streetcar to take to reach it.

She had found the shabby two-story house on Gough Street with a limp palm in a tub on the front porch. A woman in an apron and carrying a dust rag showed her the room. She was the manager, she said.

It was a small, tidy place under the eaves, furnished with an iron bed, a washstand, a chair, and a strip of rag carpet. The bathroom was on the lower floor, and the rent was two dollars and a half a week.

Rose set down her bag with a sigh of relief. That quickly, she had found herself settled in San Francisco.

Her first trip into the St. Francis Hotel had seemed just as ordinary to everyone but her. After a panic-stricken plunge into its magnificence, she was accepted without comment by the day operator, a pale girl with eyeglasses named Gladys, who was putting on her hat to leave as she gave Rose a few quick, confusing instructions.

Gladys handed Rose several unsent messages, gave her the cash box and rate book, and left. Rose sat at her desk through the evening rush of incoming guests and partygoers, into the quiet wee hours, when a few late stragglers would pass by. Occasionally one would stop at the counter to send a wire before going off to bed. Finally, at one o'clock in the morning, Rose was finished for the day.

She couldn't help thinking, as she arrived wearily back at her room, that in Mansfield, where the time was two hours later, Papa and Mama would soon be getting up to feed the chickens and horses. How different her life had become!

Rose met Gladys each day punctually at five o'clock and saw her leave. Rose rather looked forward to the moment. It was pleasant to say "Good evening" once a day to *someone*. But she suspected that if one afternoon a girl other than Rose showed up, Gladys would hardly notice.

In the afternoons before work she walked

about, looking at the city and learning to know many of the streets by name. She especially loved to walk along Hyde Street, on the top of Russian Hill. The views from there were astonishing, all the way across the bay to the east, and as far as the ocean beaches to the west, although often there was fog over the ocean. Hundreds of ships cluttered the harbor.

One day she took a streetcar out to the beach. It was colder there—much colder than in the heart of the city just a few miles away. And the weather was different as well, cloudy and misting while the sun still shone on the bay.

But here she was, at the edge of the continent, with enormous dark waves crashing on the sand, and far out across the limitless ocean the vast nations of China, Russia, and Japan. Rose shivered, as much from feeling overwhelmed by the size of the world, and how small she was in it, as from being underdressed for the cold and dampness.

She found the public library and read a

great deal. Reading had always been Rose's escape from her troubled thoughts. The library was also a pleasant place to spend Sundays, less lonely than the crowded parks. If the librarian was not too busy, Rose would sometimes talk to her about a book.

The dragging of the days, as much as her need for more money, had soon driven Rose to ask for extra work at the main office of the telegraph company. She was hired to work a shift from eight o'clock in the morning until four o'clock in the afternoon. Her new schedule left no time for anything but eating and sleeping, but there wasn't much else to Rose's life, and it allowed her to repay her debts in Kansas City and send more money back to Mama and Papa.

At the main office she had again been dropped into a desk and put down before her telegraph key, with barely a hurried human touch.

A beginner, rated at forty-five dollars a month, she replaced a seventy-five-dollar operator on a heavy wire. The days became a nerve-straining tension of concentration on the clicking sounder at her ear, while the huge room with its hundreds of instruments and operators faded from her consciousness.

Finished at four o'clock, she ate forlornly in a dairy lunchroom and hurried to the St. Francis. Here, at least, she could watch other people's lives.

Gazing out at the changing crowd in the hotel corridor, she let her imagination picture the romances, the adventures at her finger-tips. A man spoke cheerfully to the cigar boy while he lighted his cigarette at the news-stand counter. He was the center of a scandal that had filled the afternoon papers. Rose had been the operator who had sent his message to his wife, promising an explanation.

Rose also knew that the little, soft-eyed woman in clinging laces, stepping from the elevator to meet a plump man in evening dress, was there to put through a big mining deal with him. The purpose of it all was murky, but the woman's telegrams hinted at how grand the scheme was.

She was at the center of something, allowed these small peeks into the world of money and privilege. Of course, she was no more a part of it than a fly on the wall, but at least it gave her something to think and wonder about.

Rose's cramped muscles stirred restlessly. There was barely room to move in the tiny office, crowded with table and chair and waste-basket. Spaciousness was on the other side of the counter, where the music and the laughter came from.

She snatched the pencil from the counter and began a letter to Paul. Her imagination was released when she wrote letters.

Dearest Paul:

I wonder what you are doing now! It's eight o'clock and of course you've had your supper. Your mother's probably finishing up the kitchen work and putting the bread to rise, and you haven't anything to do but sit on the porch and look at the stars and the lighted windows here and there in the darkness, and listen to the breeze in the trees.

151

*And here I am, sitting in a place that looks
just like a hothouse with all the flowers come to
life. There's a ball upstairs, and a million girls
have gone through the corridors, with flowers
and feathers and jewels in their hair, and dresses
and evening cloaks as beautiful as petals.*

*How I wish you could see them all, and the
men, too, in evening dress. They're the funniest
things when they're fat, but some of the slim ones
look like princes or counts.*

*What kind of new furniture was it your
mother got? You've never told me a word about
the place you're living since you moved, and
I'm awfully interested. Do please tell me what
color the wallpaper is and the carpets, and the
woodwork, and what the kitchen is like, and if
there are rosebushes in the yard.*

*Did your mother get new curtains, too? There
is a lovely new material for curtains just out,
sort of silky and rough, in the loveliest colors.
I don't know what it's called but I see it in the
store windows, and if your mother wants me to,
I'd love to price it and get samples for her.*

A little boy's just come in with a toy balloon,

and it got away from him and it's bumping up around on the gilded ceiling, and I wish you could hear him howl. It must be fun for the balloon, though, after being dragged around for hours, tugging all the time to get away, to escape at last and go up and up and up.

I felt just like that this morning. Just think, Paul, I have paid back the first twenty dollars of the hundred dollars I owe Mama and Papa! Isn't that gorgeous? I'm making over seventy dollars a month now, with my extra work at the SF office, and my salary here.

She paused, biting her pencil. That would get his attention, she thought. He had been so smug when he had been promoted to day operator and station agent. She had not quite got over the hurt of his taking the new position without letting her know that the night operator's place would be vacant. He had explained that a girl couldn't handle the job, but she knew that he did not want her to be working with him, that he disapproved of a wife who worked.

Paul could be so old-fashioned, Rose realized. But she didn't really want to work when she was married. Her dream was to have a little house of their own, with children, and rosebushes in the yard and a dog and . . .

But there were advantages to having her own money. In the summer she would be able to get some beautiful new clothes and go home for a visit. By then she would have paid Mama and Papa back all the hundred dollars. She had decided she would not go home until she had done at least that. But she hoped to send even more, even after she'd paid them back, to help them with the farm.

When she went to Mansfield, surely Paul would come, too, when he knew she would be there. He would see then how well she could manage her money.

In a few months more she would be able to save enough for a trousseau: tablecloths, and embroidered towels . . .

"Blank, please!" A customer leaned on the counter. She gave him the pad and watched him while he wrote. His profile was handsome;

a lock of fair hair beneath the pushed-back hat, a straight forehead, an aristocratic nose, a thin, humorous mouth.

He wrote rapidly, dashing the pencil across the paper, tearing off the sheet and crumpling it impatiently, beginning again. Finally he shoved the message toward her with a quick movement, looked at her, and smiled. She felt a charm in the warm flash of his eyes. His vitality was magnetic.

Rose read the message:

C. G. Lane, Central Trust Company, Los Angeles. Drawing on you for five hundred. Must have it. Absolutely sure thing this time. Full explanations follow by letter. Gillette.

Rose counted the words. "Sixty-seven cents, please," she announced. She wished that she could think of something more to say. She would have liked to talk to him. There was about him an impression of something happening every instant. When he had paid and began to turn away, he paused. Rose looked at him quickly. But he was speaking to the operator in the next cubicle, who worked for Postal Telegraph, a competing company to Western Union.

"Hello, doll!"

"On your way," the girl replied calmly. Her eyes laughed and challenged. With an answering smile he went past, and only his hat remained visible in glimpses through the crowd. Then he turned a corner and was gone.

"Fresh!" the girl chirped. "But gee, he can dance!"

Rose looked at her with interest. She was a new girl, on relief duty for the regular operator for Postal Telegraph, a sober, conscientious woman of thirty who studied German grammar in her spare moments. This one was not at all like her.

"Do you know him?" asked Rose, smiling shyly. This was an opening for conversation, and she grabbed at it. The other girl had a friendly and engaging manner, which seemed to include all the world.

"Sure I do," she answered. She ran a slim

forefinger through the blond curl that lay against her neck, smiling at Rose with a display of even, white teeth.

Rose thought of pictures of models on magazine covers. It must be wonderful to be as pretty as that, she thought wistfully.

"Who's he wiring to?" the girl wanted to know.

Rose passed the message across the low railing that separated the offices. She noticed the shining of the girl's fingernail as she ran it along the lines.

"Well, what do you know about that? He wasn't giving me a song and dance about being Judge Lane's son. You never can tell about men," she commented wisely, returning the telegram. "Every once in a while they tell you the absolute truth."

Her comments on the passing guests fascinated Rose, now and then showing a glimpse of a world of joyousness in which the girl seemed to flutter like a butterfly in the sunshine. She worked, it appeared, only at irregular times.

"Momma supports me, of course, on her alimony. Papa certainly treated her rotten, but his money's perfectly good," she said matter-of-factly.

Her honesty was childlike, and her calm acceptance of her parents' situation made it impossible for Rose to show that she was shocked.

"She's a lot of fun, Momma is. Just loves a good time. She's out dancing now. I wish I was! I'm just crazy about dancing, aren't you? Listen to that music! All I want is just to dance all night long. That's what I really love."

"Do you often do it? Dance all night long?" Rose asked, wide-eyed.

"Only once a night." She laughed. "About five nights a week."

Rose thought her entertaining and was drawn to her beauty and charm. The girl said her name was Louise Latimer. When Louise asked Rose about her life in San Francisco, she showed astonishment at its barrenness. But she seemed to want to share her own good times. That took some of the sting out of her pity.

Why, Rose didn't know the city at all, Louise cried, and Rose could only agree. They must go out to some of the cafés together. They must have tea at Techau's. Rose must come to supper and meet Momma. Louise jumbled a dozen plans together in a rush of friendliness.

It was plain that she was touched in her butterfly heart by Rose's loneliness.

"And you're a brunette!" she cried. "We'll be stunning together. I'm so blond."

The small circle of her thoughts returned always to herself. But Rose found Louise amusing and was attracted to her light.

Rose was sure Louise would never have drifted into dull stagnation as she herself had. Louise would have found some way to fill her life with realities instead of dreams.

One o'clock came before Rose realized it. Tidying her desk for the night, she found the unfinished letter to Paul and tucked it into her purse. She had not been forced to rely upon her imagination that evening.

Louise walked to the streetcar line with her, and it was settled that the next night Rose should come to supper and meet Momma. It meant cutting short her extra work and paying the day operator to stay late at the St. Francis to cover her absence, but Rose did not regret the cost. This was the first friend the city had offered her, and she wasn't going to let Louise slip away.

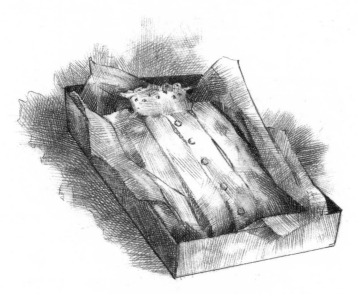

New Friends

Rose looked forward to her supper with Louise and Mrs. Latimer, but she was doubtful of herself in a strange place, with strange people. She had stopped on her way home from work and bought a new hat and a veil with large velvet spots. Yet at the very door of their apartment on Leavenworth Street, she had a moment of panic and thought of going home and sending a message of regrets. Only the thought of her desperate loneliness gave her courage to ring the bell.

Her worry disappeared as soon as she met Louise's mother. Momma, slim in a silk petticoat and a frilly dressing gown, took her in at once, with great affection.

Rose could see that Louise was much like her mother. Rose thought again of pictures on magazine covers, though Louise suggested a new magazine and her mother did not. Rose could see that Momma's pearly complexion was helped by powder, and her hair was unnaturally golden. But the eyes were the same, large and blue, fringed with black lashes. And both of their profiles had the same clear, delicate outlines.

"Yes, dear, most people do think we're sisters," Mrs. Latimer said, when Rose spoke of the resemblance.

"We have awful good times together, don't we, Momma?" Louise added, her arm around her mother's waist. Rose felt a pang at the fondness of the reply.

"We certainly do, kiddo."

It was a careless, happy-go-lucky household. Dinner was scrambled together somehow, with the opening of cans, in a neglected, dingy kitchen. Rose and Louise washed the pots and pans while Momma stirred the creamed chicken. It was fun to wash dishes again and to set the table, and Rose could imagine herself one of the family while she listened to their intimate chatter.

Momma and Louise had had tea downtown that day. There was mention of someone's new automobile, somebody's diamonds. Louise had seen a jeweled pendant called a lavalliere in a jeweler's shop. She teased her mother about buying it for her, and her mother said fondly, "Well, honey-baby, we'll see."

They had hardly begun to eat when the telephone rang. Momma, answering it in the next room, was gone for some time. They caught scraps of bantering talk and Louise wondered, "Who's that she's jollying now?"

She sprang up with a cry of delight when Momma came back to announce that the crowd was going to the beach.

Dinner was forgotten in a wink and there

was a scramble to dress. Rose, helping Louise and her mother hook the backs of their gowns in the cluttered bedroom, saw dresser drawers overflowing with sheer underwear, silk stockings, bits of ribbon, and crushed hat trimmings.

Louise brushed her eyebrows with a tiny brush, rubbed her nails with a buffer, dabbed carefully at her lips with lipstick. Rose had never used a bit of makeup. She hoped that she did not show her surprise.

They had taken it for granted that Rose was going to the beach with them. They were surprised and regretful when she said she must go to her evening job at the hotel.

"Oh, what do you want to do that for?" Louise pouted. "You look all right." She said it doubtfully, then brightened. "I'll lend you some of my things. You'd be perfectly stunning dressed up. You've got lovely hair, and that baby-blue stare of yours could be awfully cute. All you need's a dress and a little makeup—don't you think, Momma?"

Her mother agreed warmly. Rose glowed under their praise and was grateful for their interest in her. She wanted very much to go with them, and when she stood on the side-walk watching them leave in a big red auto-mobile amidst a chorus of gleeful voices, she felt chilled and lonely.

They were wonderful to be so friendly to her, she thought as she went soberly to work. She felt that she must in some way return their kindness, and after discarding a number of plans, she decided to take them both to a matinee. Then they invited her for supper again.

It was Louise, at their third meeting, who suggested that Rose come to live with them. "Do you know, Momma, Rose's living in some awful hole all alone. Why couldn't she come in with us? She could sleep in my room. Momma, why not?"

Her mother, smiling lazily, said: "Well, if you kids want to, I don't care."

Rose was so delighted, she didn't even try to talk Louise out of it. They agreed that Rose would pay one third of the expenses, and Louise cried happily: "Now, Momma, with the money we'll save, you've got to get my lavalliere!"

The next afternoon Rose packed her bag and left the room on Gough Street. Her feet wanted to dance when she went down the narrow stairs for the last time and let herself out into the windy sunshine.

Rose so looked forward to getting to know Louise and her mother better, having someone to talk to and do things with. But soon she found herself maddeningly tied down by her work.

In the early mornings, dragging herself from bed, she left Louise drowsy among the pillows. While she dressed, Rose saw the tantalizing signs of last night's entertainment— Louise's dress flung over a chair, her scattered slippers and silk stockings.

Rose came home after midnight to a dark, silent apartment. The dinner dishes were still unwashed, and she found spatterings of powder on the bedroom carpet, where street shoes and a discarded petticoat were tangled together. She enjoyed putting things in order, pretending the place was her own while she did it. But still she was lonely.

Later she awoke to blink at Louise, sitting half undressed on the edge of her bed, rubbing her face with cold cream. Rose listened sleepily to her chatter.

"You'll be a long time dead when your time comes, kiddo," Momma told her affectionately. "What's the use of being a dead one till you have to?"

Rose's youth cried that Momma was right. But she knew too well the miseries of being penniless, and she had made her promise to repay Mama and Papa first. She dared not give up either of her jobs. A remark, flung out in the endless flow of Louise's gossip, offered the solution.

"What do you know about that boob of a girl at the Merchants' Exchange office?" she said one day. "She's picked a chauffeur out of a garden of millionaires, and she's going to quit work and marry him!"

Rose's heart leaped. She would get that job.

It paid sixty dollars a month; the hours were from eight to four. It was a proper job. She could manage on that without the extra work. She could quit her second job at the central office and finally have her evenings free.

Whether she could handle market reports, which were fast and furious messages about the changing prices of cattle and oil and the like, did not even cross Rose's mind. She would figure out how to handle them. Rose had proved herself a good operator in a city that was humming with messages. Her whole nature hardened into a cold determination, and when she approached Mr. Bryant the next morning, her hands were barely trembling.

As she hoped, the job was hers for the asking. She settled into her work at the Merchants' Exchange wires with only one thought: Now she was free to live normally, to have a good time, like other girls.

The first day's work strained her nerves to the breaking point. The shouts of buyers and sellers on the floor, the impatient pounding on the counter of customers with rush messages, the whole breathless haste and excitement of the exchange, blurred into a clamor. Through the din she heard only the slow, heavy working of the wire from Chicago, where the Mercantile Exchange was located, tapping out meaningless jumbles of letters and fractions. She concentrated upon it, with an effort that made her a machine.

The scrawled quotations of prices she flung on the counter were translated from the clicking sounder at a furious pace that strained her nerves and brain. But the first day was over at last. Rose had survived it, and she hurried home.

The dim stillness of the apartment was an invitation to rest, but she disregarded it. She slipped out of her shirtwaist and splashed her face and bare arms with cold water. A new pale-green chiffon blouse she had bought in celebration of her new job was waiting in its box. A thrill of anticipation ran through her when she lifted it from its tissue wrappings.

She fastened the soft folds, pleased by the lines of her round arms seen through the transparency, and her slender neck rising from white frills. In the hand glass she gazed at the oval of her face reflected in the dressing-table mirror. Suddenly she noticed the surprising effect of the sea-blue eyes beneath her black lashes, an effect she had never known until Louise spoke of it.

She was actually pretty, Rose realized with a jolt. She was almost—she caught her breath—beautiful. The knowledge was more than beauty itself, for it brought her self-confidence. She felt equal to any situation the evening might offer.

She was smiling at herself in the mirror when Louise burst in, a picture in a dashing white serge suit and a hat whose black line was like the stroke of an artist's pencil.

"The alimony's come!" she cried. "We're going to have a regular time! Momma'll meet us downtown. Look, isn't it stunning?" She displayed the longed-for lavalliere twinkling against her smooth young neck.

"I knew I'd get it somehow. Momma—the stingy thing!—she went and got her new furs.

But we met Bob, and he bought it for me."
She sat down before the mirror, throwing off
her hat and letting down her hair.

"I don't know; it's only a chip diamond."
Her moods veered as swiftly as light summer
breezes. "I wish Momma'd get me a proper
one. It's nonsense, her treating me like a
baby. I'm seventeen."

Rose felt her delight in the new shirtwaist
waning. Louise's bright chatter, her stunning
dress and jewelry, made her feel clumsy and
slow. There was a difference between them
that they seemed unable to bridge. Rose decided that it must be her own fault. Perhaps it
was because she had been so long alone that
she hardly knew how to keep up with Louise
and her mother.

It was the same feeling she'd had in school
when she was a country girl among the town
girls. Just seeing those girls and listening to
them talk could sometimes make her feel so
much apart from the rest of the world.

This Is the Life!

The feeling of loneliness grew even stronger when Louise and Rose went out to join a crowd of Louise's friends. Rose followed Louise through a bewildering chorus of voices and music among brilliant lights and finally stumbled into a chair at a table ringed with strangers.

Momma was there, her hat dripping with plumes, white furs flung carelessly over her shoulders. Her fingers blazed with rings. There was another well-dressed woman, named Nell Allan; a bald-headed fat man called Bob; a younger man with a lean face and restless blue eyes, whom Louise greeted as Duddy.

They were having a very merry time. But Rose, shrinking unnoticed in her chair, felt isolated. She could think of nothing to say. There was no thread in the rapid chatter she could grab hold of. They were all talking, and every phrase seemed a flash of wit, since they all laughed so much.

"I love the cows and chickens, but this is the life!" Duddy cried out. "Oh, you chickens!"

"This is the life!" the others responded in a chorus of merriment.

Rose did not doubt that it all meant something, but her wits were too slow to grasp it, and the talk raced on past her. She could only sit silently, eating delicate food from plates that waiters whisked into place and whisked away again, and laughing uncertainly when the others did.

Color and light and music beat upon her brain. About her was a confusion of movement, laughter, clinking glasses, glimpses of

white shoulders and red lips, perfumes, hurrying waiters, steaming dishes. Over and through
it all wove the quick, accented rhythm of the
music, blending all her sensations into one
quickening vibration.

Suddenly, from all sides, hidden in the artificial foliage that covered the walls, silvery
bells took up the melody. Rose, speechless
and motionless, felt her nerves tingle, and she
felt alive, joyful, eager.

There was a pushing back of chairs, and
she started to get up. But they were only
going to dance, so she sat back down. Duddy
and Momma, Bob and Mrs. Allan swept out
into a whirl of white arms and dark suits,
tilted faces and swaying bodies.

"Isn't it lovely!" Rose murmured.

But Louise was not listening. She sat pout-
ing, her fingers tapping time to the music, her
eyes beneath the long lashes searching the
room. "I can't help it. I've just got to dance!"
she muttered, and suddenly she was gone,
too.

Someone met her among the tables, put his

arms around her, and whirled her away. Rose, watching for her black hat and happy face to reappear, saw that Louise was dancing with the man whose telegram had introduced them. She searched her memory until she could come up with his name. Gillette Lane.

Louise brought him to the table when the music stopped. There were cheerful introductions, and Rose wished that she could say something. But Momma monopolized Mr. Lane, squeezing in an extra chair for him beside her, and saying how glad she was to meet a friend of her little girl's. Rose listened to their confusing chatter in silence. She did not know what it was, but she thought him the handsomest man she had ever seen. She was certain that he did whatever he wanted to do with constant success.

Mr. Lane was not like the others. He talked their language, but he did not seem of them. She noticed that his hazel eyes, set in a network of tiny wrinkles, were at once eager and weary. Yet he could not be older than twenty-eight or so.

He danced with Momma when the orchestra began a rag. But coming back to the table with the others, he said restlessly, "Let's go somewhere else. My car's outside. How about the beach?"

"Grand little idea!" Duddy declared amid an approving chorus. Rose followed the others between the tables and through the swinging doors to the curb. A big gray automobile stood waiting. She told herself that she must make an effort, must pay for this wonderful evening with some contribution to the fun.

But when they had all crowded into the machine and she felt the rush of cool air against her face and saw the streetlights speeding past, she forgot everything but joy. It was her first time riding in an automobile. She was having a good time at last. A picture of the Mansfield girls flashed briefly through her mind. How meager their picnics and hay rides seemed beside this, a ride in an automobile with a group of people who would have been the scandal of her old hometown.

Rose thought of the phrases with which she would describe to Paul their racing down the long boulevard beside the beach—the salty air, the darkness, the long white lines of foam upon the breakers.

This, she realized with pleasure, was a joy-ride. She had read the phrase in newspapers, but its perfectness had never before struck her.

She was surprised, after the rush through the darkness, when the car came to a stop and everyone got out. She had thought the beach was just sand dunes and breaking waves. Amazed and trying to hide her amazement, she went with them through a blaze of light into another restaurant, where another orchestra played the same lively music and dancers whirled beyond a film of cigarette smoke.

They sat down at a round bare table, and Rose realized that everyone was ordering something to drink. She listened to the others order, hesitating.

"Blue moons" were intriguing, and "sloe gin fizzes" sounded like fireworks. Beside her

Mr. Lane said, "Scotch highball." When Rose hesitated, the waiter turned and left. Rose thought she must have done something wrong.

But when the waiter returned, he set a glass before Mr. Lane and one before her. There was a cry of "Happy days!" and Rose swallowed a queer-tasting, stinging mouthful. She set the glass down quickly.

"What's the matter with the highball?" Mr. Lane asked. He had paid the waiter, and she felt the obligation of a guest to be polite.

"It's very good really," she said. "But I don't care much for drinks that are fizzy." She saw the corners of his eyes crinkle with amusement, but he did not smile. He turned to the waiter.

"Plain highball here, no seltzer." The waiter hurried away to bring it.

Mr. Lane's attention was still upon her, and she saw no escape. She smiled at him over the glass. The waiter returned and set a new glass in front of her.

"Happy days!" she said, and drank from it.

She set down the glass just as quickly, and the muscles of her throat choked back a cough. It still tasted awful and burned her throat.

"Thank you," she croaked, and was surprised to see that the world-weariness was no longer in his eyes.

"You're all right!" he said. "I hate a bluffer who doesn't make good when he's called!" Rose didn't understand a word of what he meant, but it didn't seem to matter much. The orchestra had swung into a new tune, and he half rose. "Dance?" he asked her.

It was hard to admit it, but she said honestly, "I can't. I don't know how."

He sat back down.

"You don't know how to dance?" His keen look at her suddenly made clear something she had been trying to understand as she watched these men and women. Beneath their hilarity a game was being played, man against woman. Every word and glance was a move in that game. Rose realized that Mr. Lane thought that she, too, was playing it.

"Why do you think I'm lying to you, Mr.

Lane?" Rose asked, irritated that he could think she wasn't telling the truth. "I would like to dance if I could, of course."

"I don't get you," he replied. "What do you come out here for if you don't drink and don't dance?"

"I came because I like it," Rose said stoutly. She was too humiliated to confess her ignorance of the city in which she had lived for some months. "I've worked hard for a long time and never had any fun. And I'm going to learn to dance. I don't know about drinking. I don't like the taste of it much. Do people really like to drink highballs and things like that?"

This startled a laugh from him.

"Keep on drinking 'em, and you'll find out why people do it," he answered. Over his shoulder he said to the waiter, "A couple more Scotch highballs, Ben."

The others were dancing. They were alone at the table. Resting an elbow on the edge of it, he concentrated his attention upon her. The crowded room became a swirl of color and light about their isolation.

Rose's breath came faster. The toe of her slipper kept time to the music. Excitement mounted in her veins. Being able to hold his interest made her almost dizzy.

The highballs arrived. She did not drink hers, and when he urged, she refused as politely as she could.

"I'd really rather not," she said lightly.

"Come on, be game," he said.

"The season's closed," Rose said easily, borrowing one of Louise's sayings. "Tell me, why do people drink things that taste like that?"

"To let go, to have a good time. It breaks down inhibitions." The use of such words as "inhibitions" was one of the things that made him seem different from the others. "What's the use of living if you don't hit the high spots?"

Rose chuckled. When he asked why, she was too embarrassed to tell him. She had had a sudden picture of Mama back in Mansfield, and the look Mama would have had on her face had she been able to see Rose right then. And Paul—she felt a wave of guilt when she thought of him.

The music stopped, and the rest of their group swooped down on the table. The general ordering of more drinks ended Rose's conversation with Mr. Lane. There was a clamor of protests when Rose said she did not want anything, but Louise's momma came to the rescue.

"Let the kid alone; she's not used to it. You stick to lemon sours, baby. There's no alcohol in them. Don't let them kid you," she said. The chatter swept on, leaving Rose once more unnoticed.

But when the music called again, Mr. Lane took her out among the dancers.

"You're all right," he said, before she had a chance to protest. "Just let yourself go and follow me. It's only a walk to music."

Rose found herself dancing, felt the rhythm beat through blood and nerves. Stiffness and awkwardness dropped away from her. She felt like a butterfly bursting from its chrysalis, like a bird singing in the dawn. She was so happy that Mr. Lane laughed.

"You look like a kid in a candy shop," he said, swinging her past a jam of dancers with a long breathless swooping glide and picking up the step again.

"I'm perfectly happy!" she cried, in time to the tune. "It's aw-ful-ly good of you-ou!"

He laughed again.

She found, when she reluctantly went back to the table with him, that the others were talking of leaving. It hurt to hear Mr. Lane enthusiastically agree with the suggestion.

But after they were in the car, it appeared that they were not going home. There was more rushing through the cool darkness, and then another restaurant just like the others, and more dancing.

The hours blurred into a succession of those swift dashes through the clean night air, and then plunges into light and heat and smoke and music.

Rose, faithfully sticking to lemon sours, discovered that she could dance a rag, and something else known as a grizzly bear. She heard Duddy crying that she was some chicken, and felt herself a great success.

It wasn't until two o'clock in the morning that they sped home through the sleeping city, the stars overhead and the streetlights flashing by. Drowsily happy, Rose thought it no harm to rest her head on Mr. Lane's shoulder. She wondered what it would be like if a man so fascinating were in love with her. It would be frightfully thrilling and exciting, she thought.

"See you later!" everyone cried when she alighted with Momma and Louise before the dark apartment house. She shook hands with Mr. Lane, feeling a contraction of her heart.

"Thank you for a very pleasant time." She felt that he was amused by her polite words.

"Don't forget it isn't the last one!" he said.

Rose did not forget. The words repeated themselves, and she felt the music in her blood for a long time.

The sensations came back to her in the pauses of her work the next day. She dragged herself, wooly-headed from lack of sleep, through the hours, hearing the noise of the exchange and market quotations clicking off the Chicago wire, now very far and thin, now close and deafeningly loud.

She was white and felt limp when she got home. Momma suggested a Bromo-Seltzer and offered to lend her some rouge. But Mr. Lane had not telephoned, and Rose went to bed instead of going out with them that evening.

A Game Little Kid

The first confusion of the Merchants' Exchange had cleared a little. Rose began to see a pattern in the fluctuations of the market quotations.

January wheat, March rye, May corn became a drama to her. She snatched the figures from the wire and tossed them to the waiting boy, then saw them chalked up on the huge board. She heard the shouts of the brokers and caught glimpses of the worldwide gamble in lives and fortunes.

But she was merely a living mechanical

attachment to the network of wires. Rose did not want to work. She had never wanted to work. Working had been only a means of more quickly reaching her life with Paul. The road had run straight before her to that end.

But Paul would not let her follow it. He kept writing that she would have to wait until *he* made money enough to support her and his mother. Why couldn't she make Paul see the cozy life she herself could so clearly imagine? Why must he be so proud and stubborn?

Resting her chin on one palm, half listening to the ceaseless clicking of the sounder, she gazed across the marble counter and the vaulted room. The brokers waving their arms wildly, the scurrying messengers faded into the background.

She saw again the light and color and movement of the night when she had met Mr. Lane. She heard his voice: "What's the use of living if you don't hit the high spots?" What *was* the use? she wondered.

She decided to write a long letter to Paul, telling him honestly of her experiences.

Guiltily, she thought maybe jealousy would get him off his seat. Maybe something would change. Maybe he would finally see how foolish he was being.

The days after she mailed the letter were an agony of waiting. Restlessness took her over. She tossed and turned for hours on her pillow. When she managed to doze, she heard in her dreams the clicking of telegraph sounders, and music, and found herself dancing on the floor of the Merchants' Exchange with a strange man who had Mr. Lane's eyes.

On the eleventh day after her night out, she received a letter back from Paul that quelled the turmoil of her thoughts like a dash of cold water. In his even neat handwriting he wrote:

I suppose the folks you write about are all right. They sound mighty strange to me. I don't pretend to know anything about San Francisco, though. I don't see how you are going to hold down a job and keep up with the way they seem to spend their time, though I will not say anything about dancing. You know I could not

*do it and stay in the church. But I do not think
I would like your new friends. I would rather a
girl was not so pretty, but used less slang when
she talks.*

Paul had confidently stated an opinion that
Rose had been resisting in her thirst for
friendship and excitement. She too had had
moments of silently criticizing Louise and
Momma. But she had quickly hidden the
criticism in the depths of her mind. After all,
they were friends and had treated her with
kindness.

But now they stood revealed through Paul's
eyes as glaringly cheap and vulgar. Her longing
for a good time, if she must have it with such
people, appeared weak and foolish to her.

At the same time, Rose bristled at Paul's
judgments about folks he'd never met, and
about her. If he was so concerned about her, if
he loved her as much as he said, why couldn't
they make do as a married couple? Rose wondered how much longer Paul expected her to
be patient.

She felt older and steadier that night. Then, just as she was going to bed, the telephone rang. Louise handed the receiver to her. It was Gillette Lane, and he wanted to speak to her.

The mere sound of his voice revived the spell, and Rose gave in to it with barely a thought. Yes, she said, she would love to join the crowd tonight.

Before the dressing table, hurrying to make herself beautiful for an evening with him, Rose leaned closer to the glass and stared into her eyes, trying to find the answer to why she found him so fascinating.

"Have a heart, for the lova Mike!" cried Louise. "Give me a chance. You aren't using the mirror yourself, even!" She slipped into the chair Rose had left and, pushing back her mass of golden hair, gazed at her own face.

"Got to get my lashes dyed again; they're growing out. Say, you certainly did make a hit with Lane."

"Where's the nail polish?" Rose asked,

searching in the disorder of the bureau drawers. "Oh, here it is. What do you know about
him?"

"Well, he's one of those Los Angeles Lanes.
His father was a judge but got in trouble
for something a while ago. Loads of money."
Louise, dabbing on cold cream, spoke in jerks.

Momma, slipping a rustling gown over her
head, spoke through the folds. "He's a live
wire," she said. She settled the straps over
her shoulders, tossing a fond smile at Rose.
"Hook me up, dearie? Yes, he's a live wire
all right, and you've certainly got him interested."

A sudden thought chilled Rose to the
fingertips. She fumbled with the hooks.

"He isn't married, is he?"

"Married! Well, I should say not! What
do you think I am?" Momma demanded. "Do
you think I'd steer you or Louise up against
anything like that?"

Her voice softened. "I know too well what
unhappiness comes from someone taking another lady's husband away from his home and

family. Though he does pay the alimony regular as the day comes around, I will say that for him.

"I hope never to live to see the day my girl, or you either, does a thing like that." There were strong feelings in her voice.

Rose felt a rush of affectionate pity for her. Louise, springing up, threw her bare arms around her mother.

"Don't you worry, angel Momma! Never!" she cried.

At such moments of warmhearted sincerity, Rose was fond of them both. They were lovely to her, she thought, and they accepted people as they were, without sneaking little criticisms and feelings of superiority. At times she hardly seemed to know what she felt about anything.

Her thoughts were cut short by the squawk of an automobile horn beneath the windows. With hasty slaps of powder puffs and a snatching of gloves, they hurried down to meet Mr. Lane at the door.

Rose again felt his charm like a current

between them. But words choked in her throat, and she stood silent in a little whirlpool of greetings. Besides the driver there were three people, hard to see in the shadows, already in the automobile. A glowing cigar end lighted a fat, jolly face, and two female voices greeted Momma and Louise. Hesitating on the curb, Rose felt a warm, possessive hand close on her arm.

"Get out, Dick. Climb in back. This little girl's going in front with me."

Mr. Lane's strong voice made the words like an irresistible force. But when she was sitting beside him, and Dick had wedged himself into the crowded space behind, she asked, "Do you always boss people like that?"

They were racing smoothly down a slope, and his answer came through the rushing of the wind past her ears. "Always."

The gleam of a headlight passed across his face, and she saw it keen, alert, alive. "Ask, and you'll have to argue. Command, and people jump. It's the man who orders what he wants who gets it."

After a moment he said, more pleasantly, "Well, little girl, you haven't been forgetting me, have you?"

Rose ignored his change of tone. His idea had struck her as extraordinarily true. It had never occurred to her. She turned it over in her mind.

"A girl ought to be able to work it too," she said.

He laughed. "Maybe." Then he added, "I'm crazy about you."

"Crazy people are unaccountable," Rose quipped. Her heart was racing. The speed of the machine, the rush of the air were in her veins. She had never dreamed that she could talk like this. This man brought out something in her she had never known was there—something witty, smart, and self-assured. That knowledge made her giddy.

Mr. Lane was silent a moment, turning the automobile onto a quieter street. There was laughter behind them. One of the others called: "Go to it, Gil."

Mr. Lane did not reply, but the leap of the

car swept their chatter backward again.

"Going too fast for you?"

Rose took his words as a challenge. "I've never gone too fast!" she answered. "I love to ride like this. Where are we going?"

"Anywhere you want to go, as long as it's with me."

"Then let's just keep going and never get there," Rose said. "Do you know what I thought you meant the other night when you said we'd go to the beach?"

"No, what?"

Rose told him the mental picture she had had of a still, moonlit beach, the white breakers foaming along the shore, the salt wind, and the darkness—and the car plunging down a long white boulevard.

"Do you mean to tell me you'd never been to the beach resorts before?"

"Not in the middle of the night!" She laughed.

"You're a game little kid," he said.

She found that the words pleased her more than anything he had yet said. They sped on in silence. Rose was content just to delight in going so swiftly through a blur of light and darkness toward an unknown end.

They passed a set of park gates, and the automobile leaped like a live thing at the touch of a whip, racing faster down the smooth road between dark masses of shrubbery. A clean, moist odor of the forest mixed with a salt tang in the air. The headlights were like funnels of light cutting a space into the solid night for them to pass.

"Isn't it wonderful!" Rose sighed.

"I like the bright lights better myself," he answered. After a pause, he added, "Country bred, aren't you?"

She replied in the same tone, "College man, I suppose."

"How did you dope that?"

"'Inhibitions,'" she answered. "It's a word I'd expect to hear from a college man."

"What? O-o-oh! So you haven't been forgetting me!"

"I didn't forget the *word*," she said. "I looked it up."

"Well, made up your mind to get rid of 'em? Your inhibitions?"

"I'd get rid of anything I didn't want," Rose said.

"Going to get rid of me?"

"No," she said coolly. "I'll just let you go."

It struck her that she was utterly out of her mind. She had never dreamed of talking like that to anyone. What was she doing, and why?

"Don't you believe it one minute!" His voice had the strong ring again, and suddenly she felt that she had started a force she was powerless to control. Her only safety was silence, so she shrank back into it.

When the car stopped, she jumped out of it quickly and stood close to Momma. In the hot, smoky restaurant they found a table at the edge of the dancing floor. Rose slipped into the chair farthest from him, ordering lemonade.

Her exhilaration left her. Again she could think of nothing that seemed worth saying. She felt his amused eyes upon her while she sat looking at the red crepe-paper decorations overhead and the maze of dancing couples.

It was some time before the rhythm of the music began to beat in her blood and the scene lost its tawdriness and became cheerful.

"Everybody's dancing now!" Louise hummed, looking at Mr. Lane under her long lashes. The others were dancing, and the three sat alone at the table.

> *"Everybody's doing it, doing it, doing it.*
> *Everybody's doing it but you and me."*

They were lyrics to the music, a popular song.

"Go and grab somebody else," he answered good-humoredly. "I'm dancing with Rose, when she gets over being afraid of me." He lighted a cigarette.

"Oh, really?" Rose retorted. "I'm not afraid of you."

Then his arms were around her and they were dancing before she realized how he had tricked her. She stumbled and lost a step in her fury.

"No? Not afraid of me?" He laughed. "Well, don't be. What's the use?"

"It isn't that," she said. "Only I don't know how to play your game. And I don't want to play it. And I'm not going to. You're too clever."

"Don't be afraid," he said, and his arm tightened. She missed a step again, and lost the swing of the music.

"Let yourself go, relax," he said. "Let the music . . . That's better."

They circled the floor again, but her feet were heavy. She knew she was dancing badly, and that added to her struggle. Thoughts half formed themselves in her mind and escaped. She wanted to be able to be clear, to state her meaning in a graceful way, but she could not.

"It's this way," she said. "I'm not your kind. Maybe I talked that way for a while, but I'm not. I wish you'd leave me alone. I really do."

The music ended with a crash, and the one-two thumps of many feet echoed the last two notes.

"You really do?" His tone thrilled her with its warmth. The smile in his eyes was both soft and confident. Consciously she kept back her answering smile, looking at him as soberly as she could.

"I really do."

"All right." His quick giving in was exactly what she had wanted, but for some reason she was disappointed it had been so easy. Still, when they walked back to the table, Rose felt relieved of the burden of entertaining him and was content to watch him dance with Momma and Louise.

She crowded into the car during their quick, restless dashes from one dancing place to the next. She laughed a great deal, and when they met Duddy and Bob somewhere a little after midnight, she danced with each of them. But she decided that having a good time was almost as hard work as earning a living.

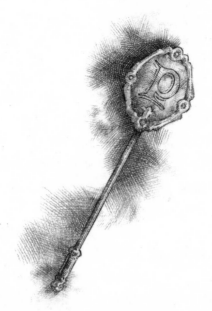

When We Are Married

It was nearly two weeks before she went out again with Momma and Louise, and this time she did not see Mr. Lane at all. Louise was astonished that he never telephoned.

"What in the world did you do with that Lane man?" she wanted to know. "You must have been an awful boob. Why, he was simply dippy about you. Believe me, I'd have strung him along if I'd had your chance. And an automobile like a palace carriage, too!" she mourned.

"Oh, well, baby, Rose doesn't know much about handling men," Momma comforted her. "She did the best she could. You never can tell about 'em, anyway. And maybe he's out of town."

But this was not true, for Louise had seen him only that afternoon with a stunning girl in a million dollars' worth of sables.

Rose was swept by crosscurrents of feeling. She told herself that she did not care what Mr. Lane did. She repeated this until she realized it wasn't her true feeling. She did care what he did, and then wondered why she cared. She hardly knew him at all.

She could picture the outside of his home only by combining the grandeur of the St. Francis Hotel with images in her mind from novels she had read. While she could see him running up grand steps, passing through a great door, and handing his coat to a dignified manservant, either a butler or a footman, her imagination could not follow him through the door, into the house.

She would have liked to know something

of his interests, but all she knew was that he liked to dance and live fast. Rose felt torn between her attraction to his playfulness and her feeling that her she should stay away from him.

She turned again to thoughts of Paul as one comes from a dark room into clear light. *This* was something she could imagine, easily and with joy: They would live in a pretty little house. There would be white curtains at the windows and roses over the porch. When the housework was all perfectly done, she'd sit on the porch, embroidering a dainty shirtwaist.

The gate would click, and Paul would come up the walk, his feet making a crunching sound on the gravel. She would run to meet him. It had been so long since she had seen Paul that his face was vague. When she finally brought from her memory the straight-looking blue eyes, the full, firm lips, the cleft in his chin, she saw how boyish he looked. He was a dear, and she truly did love him.

The days went by, most of them like the days before. Rose had volunteered to do the food marketing for the three of them and help with the cooking. She had offered because she found Louise and Momma's idea of a good solid meal wanting.

She was glad of any excuse to get out into the windy sunshine with the scent of sea always in the air. The city had so much to offer.

Along the waterfront fish sellers and their carts crowded the entrances to the wharves, crying out their days' catches in hoarse voices. The fish were laid on ice and sawdust in shimmering, multicolored piles. It amazed Rose how many different kinds and shapes of fish could be eaten.

Rose bought sea bass one trip, and red snapper another. She loved the flavor of ocean fish, so much richer and more interesting than the catfish she had often eaten at home. And Momma and Louise complimented her cooking and ate heartily.

Occasionally she would have some excitement. She saw an accident between two automobiles one day, and on another an organ grinder chasing his escaped monkey.

Once she had been walking down Market Street when she heard a deep rumble, and the earth trembled for a few seconds. A window broke in a cobbler's shop, and the trees in the park across the street swayed. It scared Rose breathless. But no one else on the street seemed to think a thing of a little earthquake. They looked up briefly and went on about their business.

Nothing had ever felt so unnatural to Rose, not even speeding along at sixty miles per hour on a jostling train. But the other operators at the exchange told her such little earthquakes happened all the time in San Francisco.

Sometimes she would walk along the streets at the edge of the Chinese district, which San Franciscans called Chinatown. Of the neighborhoods she knew, it was the most interesting. From what she could see down the side streets, it was a tiny foreign country smack in the middle of an American city. She marveled at the indecipherable signs, the bright colors, and the choppy sounds of the Chinese language. The air was thick with the exotic, spicy, and sometimes overpowering smells of cooking. The sidewalks teemed with people and produce, a stream of wide straw hats that reminded Rose of mushroom caps.

But she didn't feel comfortable actually walking through Chinatown. She didn't like to stick out in a crowd.

She found the Russian district, and a Japanese district with beautiful streets of large homes with ornate balconies and scroll-work. And she saw slums where children in tattered clothes played in the gutters.

But the pleasure of her walks, and Louise and Momma's appreciation of her cooking, were not enough. Her life was not moving forward. She had repaid Mama and Papa sixty of the one hundred dollars and wondered what she ought to do when the debt was paid.

When the fall rains began, her walks became less frequent. Every morning, in a ceaseless drizzle from gray skies, Rose rushed down a sidewalk filmed with running water and crowded onto a streetcar jammed with irritated people and dripping umbrellas.

When she reached the office, her feet were wet and cold and the hems of her skirts flapped damply at her ankles.

She had a series of colds, and her head ached while she copied endless price quotations from the ceaselessly clicking telegraph sounders. At night she rode wearily home, clinging to a strap, and crawled into bed. Her muscles ached and her throat was sore.

Momma stopped her scurry of dressing for the evening to bring her a glass of hot milk, and Rose drank it gratefully. When at last she was alone, she read awhile before going to sleep. Rose could forget the dreariness of living, swept away into a world of adventure and romance.

She passed her nineteenth birthday. Christmas came, and she recklessly spent money for gifts to send home: socks and ties and a shaving cup for Papa, a length of black silk and a ten-dollar gold piece for Mama. They made an exciting bundle, and when she stood in line at the post office, she pictured happily the delight there would be when it was opened.

Mama had written Rose asking if she couldn't come home for a visit. They hadn't seen her in a year and a half.

Rose did want to see Mama and Papa. She missed them terribly at times. She missed Rocky Ridge Farm. She wrote that she hadn't earned enough vacation to make the trip, which would require almost four days' travel just going and coming.

But the real reason Rose didn't want to go back to Mansfield was that she didn't want to have to explain why she and Paul weren't yet married. In her letters Mama hadn't asked, except to inquire if Rose had seen Paul, and how he was doing. And Rose hadn't written of her frustration with Paul.

Rose just did not want to go home without some success under her belt—success in marriage, in work, in something. She was afraid to go home before she felt she had truly escaped Mansfield. She worried that if she went home now, she might never leave.

In the meantime, she could at least get a deep satisfaction out of spoiling people with money she herself had earned.

The brokers at the Merchants' Exchange gave her a bonus of twenty dollars at Christmas. With this she bought a gilt vanity case for Louise, gloves for Momma, and Paul's present. She thought a long time about that and at last chose a monogrammed stickpin, with an old-English *P* deeply cut in the gold.

Paul sent her a celluloid box lined with puffed pink sateen, holding a comb and brush set. It made a poor showing among the flood of presents that poured in for Momma and Louise. Rose didn't care about that, but she let them think it came from her mother. She had not told them about Paul, wanting to protect that part of her life from Louise's curiosity and comments.

There were parties every night Christmas week, but Rose did not go to any of them. She was in the throes of grippe, and though the work at the office was light, it took all of her energy. Even on New Year's Eve she stayed at home, resisting all the urgings of Louise and Momma, who told her she was missing the time of her life.

She went to bed, to lie in the darkness and realize that it was New Year's Eve, that her life was going by, and she was getting nothing she wanted. "It's the man who orders what he wants who gets it." Gillette Lane's voice came back to her.

Man or woman, Rose thought, there was truth in what he had said. But she wasn't sure what she wanted, let alone how to order what she wanted.

Rain pelted the windowpanes, and through the sound of it she heard the distant uproar of many voices and a constant popping of fireworks crackling through the damp evening.

She thought of Paul. She remembered that New Year's Eve when the new century had begun. She gasped when she realized it had been exactly six years since that night. She remembered it well because that night Paul had

learned that he had gotten his first assignment as a telegraph operator, in Iowa. And it
was at that time that Rose had first realized
that she loved him.

So much had happened since then, so
much had come between them. He had been
living and growing older, too. It was impossible to see what his real life was through his
matter-of-fact letters: details of where he had
been, how much money he was saving, on
which Sundays the minister had had dinner at
his house.

Only occasional phrases were clear in her
memory. " . . . when we are married . . ." She
could still thrill over that. And he always
signed his letters "Lovingly, Paul." And once,
speaking of a Sunday-school picnic, he had
written, "I wish you had been there. There
was no girl that could come close to you."

But Paul never mentioned when they
might be married. She saw weeks and months
and maybe even years of work stretching
ahead of her like the unending row of cross-
ties in a railroad track.

On New Year's Day Rose wrote out her thoughts in a letter to Paul. She was angry and frustrated.

I don't know what to think when you can say you love me and talk of marriage. How long must we wait? What exactly are we waiting for?

She felt better after that, getting her thoughts off her chest, but decided not to mail the letter. She resolved not to mope so much. The next night she accepted Louise and Momma's invitation to go to the beach with the crowd. Bob was there, and Duddy, and many others whom Louise and Momma knew.

Again there was the stir of shifting colors under brilliant lights, the eddy and swirl of dancers, sparkling eyes, white hands, a glimmer of rings, perfume, laughter. Through it all the music throbbed and blended all sensations into one quickening rhythm, one exciting vibration of nerves and spirit.

Rose felt her weariness slip from her shoulders. She could have burst into song.

And she danced. She danced eagerly, joyously, carried by the music as by the crest of a wave. Clever remarks slipped from her lips as readily as from Louise's. She found that it did not matter what one said, only that one said it quickly. Her comments were met by applauding laughter.

In the automobile, dashing from place to place, she took off her hat and, facing the rushing wind, sang aloud for pure joy.

They ran into Gillette Lane after midnight. She turned a flushed, radiant face to him when he came over to their table. She felt sure of herself, ready for anything. He leaned past her to shake hands with Momma, who greeted him in chorus with Louise.

"Back in our midst once more!" he said to Rose over his shoulder. He brought up a chair beside hers, and she saw in his first glance that he was tired and moody. He ordered a drink and snapped his fingers impatiently until the waiter brought it.

"Who you with, Gil? Didn't see your automobile outside," said Duddy.

"Oh, I was with some crowd. Don't know where they are. Haven't got the car," he answered.

"Stick around with us then." "I bet you've been hitting the high spots, and smashed it!" Bob and Duddy said simultaneously.

But the orchestra was beginning another tune, and only Rose noticed that in the general pushing back of chairs he did not reply. She shook her head no at the question in his eyes, and he asked no one else to dance.

Of course, after that she had to refuse the others, too. They were left sitting at the bare table, ringed with the imprints of wet glasses.

A strange sadness was settling on her. She felt sorry and full of pity. She did not know why, and an impulse to put her hand on his smooth, fair hair surprised and troubled her.

"Rotten life, isn't it?" he said. It was a tone so different in him that she did not know how to reply.

"I'm sorry," she answered.

"Sorry? Good Lord, what for?"

"I don't know. I just am. I'm sorry for whatever it is that's happened to you." She saw that she had made a mistake.

She sat looking at the dancers in silence. They looked peculiar and curious, going round and round with great energy, getting nowhere. She saw the perspiring musicians working wearily, with glances at the clock.

"Funny," she said at length.

"What?"

"All these people, and me too, doing this kind of thing. We don't get anything out of it. What do we do it for?"

"Oh, it's just a safety valve from the burden of life." His voice was very tired.

The more she considered the idea, the more her admiration for him grew. She was not in the least afraid of him now. She was eager to talk to him. Somehow, oddly, it seemed they had something in common. They were both outside the circle of fun that was going on around them.

Gillette stood up and Rose unthinkingly put

out her hand to stay him. But he ignored it.

"So long," he said carelessly, and she saw that, absorbed in some thought, he hardly knew that she was there.

She let him go and sat turning an empty glass between her fingers, lost in her wondering about him.

Though she spent many of her evenings at the beach during the next several weeks, she did not see him again, and she heard one night that he had had a business reversal and left town.

She could not believe that disaster had conquered him. Her mind returned frequently to him, drawn by an irresistible fascination. It could not be that she loved him. Could it?

A Surprise Visit

One day, a month or so into the new year, Rose had a rough day at the office. A mistake had been made in a message. A furious broker, saying that it had cost him thousands of dollars, said that Rose was at fault. He was going to sue the telegraph company and had pounded the counter and refused to be quieted.

All day Rose felt disaster looming. It would be months before the error was traced. She racked her brain trying to remember if she had sent the right word—did she really click "sell" instead of "buy"? But she couldn't be sure.

Dots and dashes jumbled together in her mind. She was exhausted at four o'clock and thought eagerly of a hot bath and the softness of her pillow. Slumped in the corner of the cable car, she endured its jerks and jolts, keeping a grip on herself until the moment when she could relax.

Louise was hanging over the banister on the upper landing when she entered the hall of the apartment house. Her excited whisper met Rose on the stairs.

"Somebody's here to see you," she hissed.

"Who?" Rose wondered. It was unusual enough that anyone should just drop in to see Rose. Pictures of Mama and Papa, accidents and deaths, flashed through Rose's startled mind.

"He said his name was Cooley," Louise whispered. "He's an awful stick-in-the-mud. Momma sent me out to give you the high sign. That American Beauty makeup salesman is in town," she rushed onward. "There's going to be a party at the Cliff House. You could sneak to your room and dress, and we could beat it out the back way.

"Momma is talking with the guy in the living room. She'll get rid of him somehow. You can fix it up afterward."

The news stunned Rose. Her first thought was that Paul must not see her looking like this, disheveled, her hair untidy, and her fingers ink stained. Her heart was beating fast, and there was a fluttering in her wrists.

It was incredible that he was really near, separated from her only by a door. The picture of him sitting there, suffering with Momma's efforts to entertain him, was awful.

She tiptoed in breathless haste past the closed door and to the safety of the bedroom, Louise's kimono rustling behind her.

Rose's first glance into the mirror gave her a shock. She tore off her hat and coat and let down her hair with trembling fingers.

"He's a very good friend," she explained

to Louise. "I must see him. Heavens! What a fright! Be an angel and find me a clean shirt-waist," Rose whispered.

The comb shook in her hand; hairpins slipped through her fingers; the shirtwaist she found lacked a button, and every pin in the room had disappeared.

It was an eternity before she was ready, and then, leaning for one last look in the glass, she was still dissatisfied. There was no color in her face. Even her lips were only palely pink. She bit them till they reddened. Then she rubbed her cheeks with a bit of Louise's rouge pad. That was better. Just another touch of powder. There!

"Do I look all right?"

"Stunning! Aw, Rose, who is he? You've never told me a word." Louise was wild with curiosity.

"Later," Rose said. She drew a deep breath at the living-room door. Her little-girl shyness had come back upon her. Then she opened the door and walked in.

Momma, in her kimono, was sitting in the

darkest corner of the room, with her back toward the window.

Paul sat facing her, in a stiff chair. He stood to meet Rose.

"Good afternoon, Paul," Rose said, embarrassed by everything: the untidy apartment, Momma's kimono, and her own appearance.

"Good afternoon." They shook hands.

"I'm very glad to see you. Won't you sit down?" Rose heard herself saying. Momma rose, clutching her kimono around her.

"Well, I'll be going, as I have a very important engagement, and you'll excuse me, Mr. Cooley, I'm sure," she said mischievously. "So charmed to have met you," she added with artificial sweetness. Paul nodded his head.

The closing of the door behind her left them facing each other with nothing but awkwardness between them. Paul had changed in some way Rose couldn't put her finger on, though the square lines of his face, the honest blue eyes, the firm lips were as she remembered them.

Under the smooth-shaven skin of his cheeks there was the blue shadow of a stubborn beard. He looked prosperous in a well-made broadcloth suit, but not quite sure of himself. He held a black derby hat in his left hand.

"I'm awfully glad to see you," Rose finally managed to say. "I'm so surprised! I didn't know you were coming."

"I sent you a telegram," he replied. "I wasn't sure until last night that I would come."

"I didn't get it," she said. Silence hung over them like a threat. "I'm sorry I didn't know. I hope you didn't have to wait long. I'm glad you're looking so well. How is your mother?"

"She's all right. How is yours?"

"She's very well, thank you." Rose felt herself nearly hysterical with nerves. "Well, how do you like San Francisco weather?"

Paul's bewilderment faded slowly into a grin.

"It *is* rather hard to get started," he admitted. "You look different than I thought you would, somehow. But I guess we haven't changed much really. Can't we go somewhere else?"

She saw his dislike of the house in the look he cast at the living room. It was natural, Rose thought. But she did feel a loyalty to Momma and Louise.

That room with its close air, its film of dust over the tabletops, its air of neglect with the open candy box on the piano stool and the sooty papers in the gas grate was still much pleasanter than the place where she had been living when she met Louise.

"I don't know just where," she replied. "Of course, I don't know the city very well because I work all day. But we might take a walk. I'll get my coat and hat."

There was a scurry in the hallway when she opened the door. She caught a glimpse of Louise in petticoat and corset cover dashing from the bathroom to the bedroom. Rose grabbed her coat and hat without a word to Louise. Then she led Paul quickly out the door.

Paul said he could not stay in town long,

only twenty-four hours. He wanted to see the superintendent personally about a plan to put in a spur track at Sacramento for the loading of melons. Rose's thoughts did not follow his business chatter. She heard something about irrigation districts and water feet and sandy loam soil.

So he had not come to see her! Then Rose saw that he, too, was talking only to cover a sense of strangeness and embarrassment as awkward as her own.

She wished that they were comfortably sitting down somewhere where they could talk. It was hard to say anything interesting while they walked along bleak streets with the wind snatching at them.

"Whew! You certainly have some wind in this town!" he exclaimed. At the top of Nob Hill its full force struck them, whipping her skirts and tugging at her hat while she stood gazing down at the gray honeycomb of the city and across it at masses of sea fog rolling over Twin Peaks.

"It gives me an appetite, I'll tell you!

Where'll we go for supper?"

Rose hesitated. She could not imagine his being comfortable in any of the places she knew. Music and brilliant lights and cabaret singers would be another barrier between them added to those she longed to break down.

She said that she did not know the restaurants very well, and his surprise reminded her that she had written him pages about them.

She fell to talking about her work. Surely that was a safe subject. But she quickly saw that he did not like this either. He said that it was a rotten shame she had to do it.

They found a small restaurant downtown. After he had hung up his hat and they had discussed the menu, she sat turning a fork over and over and wondering what they could talk about.

"Look here, Rose, why didn't you tell those folks where you live that we're engaged?" Paul asked suddenly. He wasn't demanding, but the words were a shock to Rose. She straightened in her chair, and her mind raced to defend herself.

"Why . . ." How could she explain her vague feeling about keeping her private life safe from Louise and Momma? "Why, I don't know. What was the use?"

"What was the use? Well, for one thing, it might have cleared things up a little for some of these other fellows who know you."

What had Momma told him? "I don't know any men who would be interested," she said.

"Well, you never can tell about that," he answered. "I was sort of surprised, that's all. I had an idea girls talked over such things."

She was tired, and the warmth of the restaurant, and the calmness of his voice lulled her to carelessness.

"I suppose they do," she said smartly. "They usually talk about their rings." Suddenly she realized what she had said and was filled with regret. Paul's cheeks grew dully red.

"I didn't mean—" she began, the words clashing with his.

"If that's it, I'll get you a ring," he said quickly.

"Oh, no! No! I don't want you to. I wouldn't think of taking it." Rose felt terrible.

"Of course you know I haven't had money enough to get you a good one," Paul said matter-of-factly. "I thought about it pretty often, but I didn't know you thought it was so important. Seems to me you've changed an awful lot since I knew you."

Rose's apology and explanation stuck in her throat. What he said was true. She had changed. They had both changed so much that they might be strangers.

"Do you really think so?" she asked sorrowfully.

"I don't know what to think," he answered with pain in his voice. "I've been thinking about things, about the things you wrote, and wanting to see you again. And now, I don't know, you seem so different, sitting there with paint on your face."

Her hand flew to her cheek as if she had been slapped.

"And talking about rings. You didn't use to be like this a bit, Rose," he went on earnestly. "It seems to me as if you'd completely lost track of your better self somehow. I wish you'd—"

Rose felt her dander getting up. Her "better self" indeed!

"Please don't begin preaching at me!" she interrupted. "I'm perfectly able to take care of myself. Really, Paul, you just don't understand. It isn't anything, really, a little bit of rouge. I only put it on because I was tired and didn't have any color.

"And I didn't mean it about the ring. I just didn't think what I was saying. But I guess you're right. I guess neither of us knows the other anymore."

She felt desolate. Everything seemed all wrong with the world. She listened to Paul's assurances that he knew she was all right, whatever she did, that he didn't care anyhow, that she suited him.

But his words sounded hollow in her ears, for she knew that beneath them was the same uncertainty she felt. When he said again that he would get her a ring, she answered that she did not want one, and they said no more about it.

He left her at her door promptly at the proper hour of ten. As they stood there, unsure what to say, she reached out and grasped his hands in hers. She felt suddenly that they had taken hold of the situation by the wrong end somehow, but that everything would be all right if they could only have a chance.

Paul felt the same way. "I don't suppose you could take the morning off," he said. "I have to see the superintendent, but maybe we could manage an hour or two."

"No," Rose said. "I have to work." This would not be the chance. With the problem of the missent message hanging over her, she dared not further spoil her record by taking a day off without notice. And she knew that one or two hours more could not possibly make up the distance between them.

"Well, good night," Paul said quietly.

"Good night," Rose answered. Their hands

clung a moment and dropped apart. If only he would say something, do something, she did not know what. But awkwardness held him as it did her.

"Good night." The broad door swung slowly shut behind her. Even then she waited a moment, with a wild impulse to run after him. But she climbed the stairs instead and went wearily to bed, her heart aching with loss.

What had happened to them? Where had it all gone wrong?

Life Begins Anew

In the morning Rose was exhausted. She had barely slept the night before. She drove herself through the day's work and wondered if she had ever loved Paul. She thought she had, but she felt so much older now that it was hard to remember what she had felt in the past, and whether any of it was real.

"'Unless you can love, as the angels may, With the breadth of heaven betwixt you,'" she murmured, remembering a volume of poetry she had found on a library shelf in

Kansas City. She had thrilled over it when she had read it, dreaming of Paul. Now it seemed to her almost cruel. She would never have guessed when she was younger how difficult life would be for her as an adult.

Maybe she would have a lifetime of work. Her aunt Eliza Jane had worked most of her life as a bachelor girl before she married. Rose saw years of effort ahead of her, but then she determined that she would accumulate money enough to buy a little house of her own.

There would be no one in it to criticize her choice of friends or say that she painted her face. That remark of Paul's clung like a burr in her mind. She wouldn't mind a lifetime in which no one would have the right to say things like that!

That feeling helped raise her spirits. Louise and Momma were going out, and she decided to go with them. They said they had never seen her in a better mood.

She went again the next night. She began to go almost as often as Momma and Louise, and to understand the restlessness that drove them. This life of Louise and her mother's, racing from dissatisfaction to dissatisfaction, wasn't for her, she knew. But it would do until she got a better idea.

"What's the matter, little one? Got a grouch?" said Louise's new boyfriend, the American Beauty cosmetics salesman, one night. He was jovial and bald. His neck bulged over the back of his collar, and he wore a huge diamond on his little finger.

"Not a bit!" Rose laughed. "Only for some reason I feel like a cold plum pudding."

If Gillette Lane were only here, she thought, sinking back into herself, the sparkle of life would come back for her. She would be exhilarated, witty, alive to her fingertips once more. She knew she could never love him, but she enjoyed his company. He was different from the others.

The crowd was moving on again. Rose went with them into the cool night. Squeezed into a corner of the automobile, she sat in silence, and it was some time before she noticed the note of excitement in the others.

Louise's boyfriend was shouting, "Give her the gas! Let her out! Dash it, if you let 'em pass!" The machine fled like a runaway thing. Against a blur of sand dunes Rose saw a long gray auto creeping up beside them.

"You're going to kill us!" Momma screamed.

The gray car was forging past them. It swerved. Momma's scream was torn to ribbons by the wind. It was ahead now, and one yell from its driver came back to them. Their speed slowed.

"He says he's turning in at The Tides. Stop there?" the chauffeur asked over his shoulder.

"Yes, of course! Wha'd yuh think you're driving, a baby carriage?" the car's owner raged. They pulled into the restaurant beside the gray car.

Rose stumbled from the running board and bumped against Gillette Lane.

"Good Lord, were you in that car?" he cried. "Some race!" Then he added, "Come on in with us. This night is on me!"

Inside they ordered their drinks, helter-skelter, in a clamor. Rose sat next to Gillette, basking in the glow of his self-confidence.

"What's the big idea?" someone asked him. "You look like you've got a tiger by the tail."

"Better than that," Gillette said heartily. "I've got hold of the biggest proposition that ever came down the pike. Thousands of acres of land, good land, that'll raise anything from heaven to breakfast."

Rose listened, enraptured.

"Do you know what people are paying for land in California right now?" he went on. "I'll tell you. Five hundred, six hundred, a thousand dollars an acre. And I've got thousands of acres of land sewed up down south in the San Joaquin Valley.

"Do you know what I got from the best real estate firm on the coast? An unlimited letter of credit! Get that—'unlimited'? From Stine and Kendrick, the big real estate brokers down in San Jose. I'm going to be rolling in velvet!"

"Oh, Gil!" Rose cried. "That's wonderful!"

Everyone else cried out in approval.

"It's the biggest land proposition ever put out in the West! Ripley Farmland Acres! I'm going to put them on the map in letters a mile high! Believe me, I'm going to wake things up! There's half a million in it for me if it's handled right, and believe me, I'm some handler!"

He was full of radiant energy and power. Rose's imagination leaped to grasp the bigness of this project. Thousands of lives changed, thousands of families migrating, cities, villages, railroads built.

The music called, and Gil led Rose out onto the dance floor. They danced together on the waves of rhythm, his arms around her.

"I'm mad about you!" Gillette said, his face close to hers.

"Don't be," Rose said, pulling back. "You're wasting your time."

"And why is that?" he asked.

"First of all, I don't love you," she said. Gil made a face. "And secondly, I have begun to think I'm not the marrying type. I seem to fancy my independence."

He laughed. "You just haven't met the right fellow. So what will you do in the meantime? I don't even know what kind of work you do."

Rose was almost embarrassed to tell him. He was a man of grand schemes, and Rose was only a tiny link in the great web of wires that connected the country.

"I'm an operator for Western Union. At the Merchants' Exchange. Nothing to talk about, really. Just a bachelor girl like a thousand others."

The music stopped, and they decided to go back to the table while the others danced to the next tune.

When they sat down, Gil looked at Rose with sober eyes. "You're better than that," he said. "You've got a quick mind, a good wit. There's something . . . intelligent about you. I could use someone like you down in the valley. I'll bet you'd make one heck of a good land salesman."

"Oh, I can't take you seriously!" Rose said. Yet she felt a fluttering in her stomach.

"I mean it. I've got to hire a whole crew of salesmen. You've got to come along. You'll get rich, and you'll make me richer along the way. If you hated it, you could come right back here and probably get your job back. What do you say?"

"I'm dreaming," said Rose, not believing a thing he said. "Since when do women sell real estate?" She knew nothing of real estate, but she guessed it was a man's world.

"Since I said so." His voice became serious.

Behind the craziness of it all, Rose had a growing feeling of excitement. The careful, plodding life she had known might be about to end. Change and opportunity could be ahead.

Gillette's nearness, his voice, the light in his eyes, were all that she had been wanting, without knowing it, all these months. The music stopped with a crash.

In a flash Rose remembered the last time she had seen him and the dreary months that had followed.

"All right," he said. "It's settled?"

"You really think I could do it?" Rose said, still unsure.

"I really do." His eyes were on hers, and she saw his confidence shine out. "You will!" he said.

"Let's talk this over a little while by ourselves, Gil. Where it's less noisy," she said hurriedly.

"Not on your life! It's settled. You're coming south with me tomorrow. You'll see. It'll be the best thing that ever happened to you."

Rose's head spun as Gil announced to the crowd that Rose was going to come to work with him selling land.

Louise and Momma were upon her with excited cries and kisses. Rose, flushed, laughing, trying to keep her wits, heard Gil's voice ordering drinks and answering questions.

Rose knew then that she really was going to sell land with Gil. The knowledge left her trembling with excitement.

She was happy to be going somewhere new, and she couldn't help thinking that she was following a family tradition. How often she had heard Mama and Papa and Eliza Jane talk about the settling of Dakota Territory when they were all young.

Man's thirst for fertile land was eternal, Rose thought. It was in the blood, and especially in the blood of her family. They had settled the prairie all those years before, seeking a dream of self-reliance and prosperity. Now it was Rose's turn.

She was going to help settle California's great estates. Gil had explained to her that the huge Mexican grants of land from the old days were now being passed to the second and third generations. They were being broken up and sold off under the pressure of growing population and increased land taxes. For the first time in the state's history the land hunger of the poor man could be satisfied.

Late that night, after Gillette had dropped them all back at the apartment, Rose hurriedly packed her things. She would have to leave the apartment early to meet Gillette at the depot. Momma had gone straight to bed, after saying good-bye to Rose and wishing her all the luck in the world.

Louise sat on her bed watching Rose fold her clothes and pack the telescope bag.

"Oh, Rose," she said in a dreamy voice. "It's so romantic, the way he just swept you off your feet."

"I'm only going to work for him, Louise. I'm not marrying him."

"But you will," Louise declared, kicking off her shoes. "It's in his eyes. He loves you. And you like him well enough, don't you?"

"I don't know if I do," Rose replied. "All I know is that what he's offering has to be better than what I'm doing now, which is waiting for something to happen. I'm tired of waiting."

In that instant Rose realized that when she boarded the train in the morning, she would be truly her own person. The ache she had long felt about Paul was being replaced by self-confidence and hope for the future. She made a vow to herself to go home to

Mansfield for a visit as soon as she could manage. She could do that now, and she could stand the questions about Paul and the marriage that she knew would never take place. The thought of finally seeing Mama and Papa again made her lighthearted, and she began to whistle.

Already she could feel her life beginning anew. She could not wait for what the future would bring.